Beyond Possession
(The Afterlife Series Book 4)
By Deb McEwan

The right of Deb McEwan to be identified as the author of this work has been asserted by her in accordance with the Copyright, Designs and Patents Act 1988.

This is a work of fiction. While some places and events are a matter of fact, the characters are the product of the author's imagination and are used in a fictitious manner. Any resemblance to actual persons, living or dead, is purely coincidental.

Cover Design by Jessica Bell

In loving memory of
James Craig Brack
4 May 1998 to 25 September 2017
Gone, but not forgotten

Author's Note

Thanks for choosing 'Beyond Possession', book four in my Afterlife Series. If you haven't read the first three books ('Beyond Death', 'Beyond Life' and 'Beyond Destiny') I recommend you read them before this one. Here's a summary of the story so far.

Big Ed has coerced three teenage girls into accompanying him to a party with the offer of free food and booze. They're unaware they will be groomed to have sex with older men. Melanie smells a rat, changes her mind and leaves the car before it reaches its destination.

Claire Sylvester dies in a RTA the morning after the best night of her life, along with Ron, her taxi driver. Her twin brothers Tony and Jim know she's dead before being told.

An angel named Gabriella tell Claire and Ron there's a backlog of souls waiting to be processed due to a natural disaster on earth. They're kept at Cherussola until the Committee decide their future, but are allowed to visit their friends and family. Claire discovers that her fiancée had a one-night stand with her best friend, and that her parents' marriage is a sham. Her father has been living a double-life for many years and she has a half-sister called Melanie. She also discovers she can communicate with her brothers and that she has powers that many dead souls do not.

Ron discovers his wife had an affair with Ken, his former boss. Ken dies and goes to Hell. He is reincarnated in different forms and his soul is in constant fear and pain.

Claire's mother Marion and Ron's wife Val meet by chance and join a charity. At a get together Tony meets Val's daughter Libby; they become romantically involved.

Val is already in a delicate state due to her husband's death. She is mugged (by three humans and one evil soul) during a training course and Ron begs Claire to do everything in her power to bring the muggers to justice. They discover where the muggers live and hang out, then hatch a clever plan to catch the muggers, involving Claire's twin brothers and Jim's girlfriend Fiona.

Melanie's friends tell her about their ordeal so she informs the police. Big Ed and his accomplice Sandy kidnap her. Claire helps her brothers to find and save Melanie, but Big Ed escapes along with Sandy. He loses his temper and kills Sandy.

Having observed Claire and Ron's work with the twins, the Committee inform Gabriella that Claire is to remain where she is for a while to help people, while the angels are busy dealing with the backlog. Ron has the choice of whether to remain with Claire, or to move on to eternity. Claire is sent back to Earth to visit her family and friends, not knowing whether Ron will be in Cherussola when she returns.

On her pleasant journey upwards Sandy feels a rough jolt. The Committee have decided that she was complicit in Big Ed's crimes so must go to Hell. The decision causes a disagreement and Gabriella's brother is removed from the Committee by his mother Amanda.

Sandy suffers torture, and humiliation in Hell but refuses to cooperate with the demons. They return her to Earth to suffer in many different guises. The Committee eventually relent and save her between reincarnations.

Unable to return to Cherussola, Claire spends time watching her family and friends. Tony and Libby marry in Gretna Green while their mothers are in Zambia, working in an orphanage for their charity. When Gabriella returns Claire to Cherussola, she introduces her to Sandy. Ron decides he wants to stay with Claire and look out for his wife Val, so delays his journey to heaven. Claire ensures that Libby knows her father watched her wedding.

Big Ed, now calling himself Gary, has fled the country and had cosmetic surgery to alter his looks. He is still supplying men with young girls but has a legitimate building business for cover. Marion and Val meet him while in Zambia. Val is instantly attracted to him but Marion has a bad feeling – the women fall out but Marion's instincts prove to be correct. Girls go missing from the orphanage, some presumed dead from animal attacks.

Claire meets the angel Raphael who is Gabriella's twin. The attraction is mutual.

Claire's father Graham overcomes his many problems and turns his life around by becoming a body-builder. His ex girlfriend Carol softens and they eventually get back together.

Claire has a near miss and is saved from Hell by Raphael, Gabriella and some others. Back home Gabriella explains that Claire is being recruited to help the fight against evil. She explains how some evils are contained in a hard to access cave known by the locals as Hell on Earth. A number of evil souls in the guise of cockroaches are watched over by angels, disguised as bats.

Jim and Fiona marry and Tony and Libby receive a blessing at the same time.

With help from the angels and spirits, Big Ed is eventually caught and jailed for his heinous crimes. He meets an untimely death in a foreign prison and is sent to Hell.

Claire, her angel lover Raphael and his mother try to avoid Hell's gates while fighting the demons. While they are preoccupied, serpents amass outside the cave know as Hell on Earth.

Val is depressed and struggles to come to terms with the humiliation and shame of being involved with Big Ed who she knows as Gary. She starts to self-harm, then attempts suicide.

Gabriella mounts a rescue mission to bring back her mother, brother and Claire from the gates of Hell.

The angels are busy and the evils take advantage. Evils are sent to the cave known as Hell on Earth, in the form of serpents, to release other evil souls from their prison. While many evils are at the cave working on the escape, the angel Zach is able to escape from Hell. He meets Claire and the others involved in the rescue attempt. Claire is ordered to return to Cherussola with Zach, while Gabriella and the host attempt to rescue her mother and brother.

Harry, Big Ed's son, escapes from the cave. He needs help to avenge the wrongs against him so goes to in search of his father.

After a number of reincarnations as a lap dog, the evils eventually claim Big Ed. He is taken to his rightful home in Hell. After his initiation, his masters recognise him as one of their own and realise his strength. Some try to get on his side, knowing it's only a matter of time before he becomes their superior. When he's strong enough he punishes those who tortured him when he first arrived.

The twins are headhunted by the staff from the secret school for people with special abilities (SAP School). They are recruited and have to pretend they work for a different organisation.

Big Ed is determined to seek revenge against a number of people still living. He meets with Harry and issues orders. Harry obeys without question, knowing his son will eventually become more powerful. Until he does, Big Ed has to carry out menial tasks to learn his trade and to build his strength.

Marion dreams that Melanie is attacked. She visits Carol and they hear Melanie scream. They rush her to hospital after she is attacked by a vicious, otherworldly spider. Past events are put to bed as Marion forgives Carol and becomes close to Melanie, Claire's half sister.

Though still in pain, Raphael notices his torture is now random. He is able to look around, and realises a number of senior evils are missing. His mother transmits her thoughts, telling him it is time to escape. They do so, taking some misplaced good souls with them.

Following selection, Tony and Jim carry out various roles for the school. Their wives are suspicious, more so Fiona who is eventually recruited.

When Marion and Libby go to collect Val from hospital they meet her psychiatrist, Dr Basil Walters. This is life changing for Marion and the doctor.

Claire has to decide how to fight the evils, not knowing whether the other angels will return. Zach wakes up and although he is a senior angel, it is obvious that his time in Hell has affected him. Claire notices his scars and broken body. She formulates a plan to help fight the evils and recruits Ron and Sandy. Zach is not back to full fitness and can only give limited assistance.

Raphael returns to Claire, broken. He sleeps for what seems like an eternity and she wonders if he will ever wake up.

Graham travels to weight-lifting competitions so Marion spends more time with Carol and Melanie. Val believes that Gary is visiting her dreams and Libby discovers this when she rooms with her mother during one of Mel's visits.

The Committee are too busy to hear Claire's ideas so she decides to go ahead with her plan, without their permission.

Various attempts to discover details about the SAP School are thwarted. The twins' training is intensified as the staff want to know whether their communications with their dead sister could assist in the fight against crime.

The evils are becoming more organised and are starting to win the battle against good.

After a period of peace, Val's nightmares return and become worse. She knows that Gary is in her head when she's asleep. As well as being terrified, it's driving her insane.

Marion has a secret relationship with Basil, not yet ready to tell her family about him. While she's away, Melanie has nightmares involving Big Ed.

Big Ed practises his possession techniques. Once he's satisfied he can overcome any hosts, he sets out to find an evil person who he can bring into line.

Claire has a run-in with an evil known as Goth who later escapes. When they next meet she transforms Goth's body into a Cockroach. Goth has arranged a surprise for Claire's brothers so Claire has to leave her before being able to transform her head.

Big Ed possesses mad Martin, the country's most notorious serial killer, during a prison transfer. He escapes and commits further murders. Eventually, Big Ed dominates him and he is forced to go along with his plans. Big Ed, now in the body of Mad Martin goes to claim Val.

Gabriella and Amanda return to work and Claire is promoted to angel while on a mission. With Gabriella's help they find Goth-Roach, turn her head into a roach and deliver her to the cave.

Claire sleeps on return to Cherussola and is awoken by Raphael. He is scarred and damaged but is going to get better.

Claire, Gabriella, Raphael, Zach and Ron watch as Mad Martin heads for Marion's apartment, buoyed on by the voice in his head. Val is home alone as he enters the house and makes his way to her bedroom. When he speaks, Val knows that Gary has taken over his mind and body. He walks toward her carrying a knife and she backs towards the window, opening it she climbs out onto the ledge. He joins her and Val embraces him, then jumps. Libby and Tony pull up in their car in time for Libby to see her mother and the man landing on the concrete.

As Claire is transforming Big Ed, a dark invisible presence arrives and drags him and Mad Martin away. The Devil doesn't show himself but torments the souls until they can take no more. He then shows himself and destroys them permanently. When he'd finished with them, the Devil turns to Claire and undresses her with his eyes, before putting a hand on her shoulder and pushing her downwards. He starts to torture her as he pushes her further down towards his home. As she loses hope, Claire hears the voice of the Lord. She feels warmth on her body and the Devil's mark disappears from her shoulder.

The Lord and Devil fight until the Devil returns to Hell with his tail between his legs, vowing to win the next round.

And now book four.

Chapter 1

Between Heaven and Earth, Val waited in Cherussola as instructed. She knew she should be grateful at the chance of redeeming herself in another life, but was terrified. The best of her previous life was her wonderful children Libby and Carl; she considered the rest a disaster and had no desire for repetition. So overwhelmed by the fear of the unknown Val almost forgot about being rejected by Ron, recalling the way he'd floated away to meet his new love Sandy. Almost, but not quite. It seemed that even in death, life was unfair. She'd been weak, but had killed two birds with one stone by taking the evil serial killer Mad Martin to his death along with Gary who'd occupied his body. Everyone else knew him as Big Ed, but to Val he would forever be Gary. Yet still she wasn't considered good enough to move on to a better place and would have to endure another life to be unknowingly tested and judged. Her fear was making her feel tired and her true self outed. She felt bitter and hard done by wanting her new spirit world to go away. She also yearned to be with Ron but that was another of the many disappointments she would have to deal with.

As the angels Gabriella and Zach approached, Gabriella sensed Val's bitterness. Many would love a new chance at life to be able to redeem themselves or be given the opportunity to help others. Gabriella was disappointed at Val's sense of entitlement and wondered briefly if a short spell in Hell might have improved her attitude. She berated herself as the atmosphere changed due to her dark thoughts. She suddenly stopped mid air.

'Gabriella! What on...' Zach pulled himself up short but still had to dodge around her to avoid a collision. 'What's up, old thing?' he asked.

He seemed to have no idea. Gabriella was amazed he couldn't detect Val's bitterness and her own troubled thoughts. She reminded herself he was now the boss and her mentor. She worried about the future. Ignoring his comment she concentrated on calming herself, knowing that her thoughts could turn to reality and make life worse for many souls, both in Cherussola and on Earth. Not strictly true, she corrected herself. Before her demotion that would have been the case but now some of her powers had been taken away, she wasn't quite sure.

'I'm sorry, Zach. Everything's fine now.'

'But what's wrong?'

'I wondered whether Val would make the most of her new life and got to overthinking, that's all. I'm not sure whether...'

'It's the right decision, Gabriella, you mark my words. Now let's get a move on.'

He'd become more business-like since his promotion so it was pointless arguing. The Committee were adamant that Gabriella, her brother Raphael and their mother Amanda were to be kept under a tight rein. Their mentors who doubled as bosses were determined to prove themselves to the Committee, but Zach's attitude did seem somewhat over the top. She tried to lift her dark mood as they arrived at Cherussola. It must have worked as she noticed Val's attitude change and could sense she felt the usual warm glow at their presence. One of the wonderful perks of being an angel.

Val wondered if every soul felt this when they knew it was time to go. Feeling composed and slightly less stressed she looked at the angels and voiced the question asked by those who had come before. Most considered themselves the lucky ones; good enough for a second chance.

'What do you want me to do?'

'I want you to live a good life,' said Gabriella. Zach gave a little cough so she took the hint.

'Quite. Live a good life as the lady said, but there's more to it. Do the right thing. Whenever you're unsure and temptation rears its ugly head, listen to your conscience. It'll show you the right path and all you need to do is take it,' said Zach.

'And,' said Gabriella. 'Be kind to others and do unto them...'

'Thank you for your input, Gabriella,' said Zach, thereby silencing his assistant as he now thought of her. 'Val, be kind to others whether or not they're kind to you.'

They both smiled serenely at her, though neither felt particularly serene at that moment.

Val attempted a smile while trying to hide her terror.

Gabriella was about to ask whether she was ready, when Zach put a hand on her arm to silence her.

'Are you ready?' he asked and Val nodded

'Say goodbye to Val and close your eyes.'

'Where am I going?'

'All will become clear in time. Goodbye.'

She did as bid. Like all other second chancers, Val saw stars on a black background, spinning around inside and outside of her head. Their number multiplied and she started to feel dizzy. The black background became smaller and smaller as the stars blurred seeming to join together. All she could see wherever she looked was one intensely bright light, and it called to her. Her fear had now disappeared as Val headed towards the light.

Zach and Gabriella watched as the hospital scene opened up before them. A woman was panting heavily as she held her husband's hand in the labour ward. Their viewing was interrupted by a whoosh. Amanda appeared in front of them. 'The Committee want to talk to you, Gabriella.'

'Do they want me?' asked Zach.

'They want you to place Val's soul, Zach. I've just been asked to bring Gabriella.'

Gabriella could see her mother was irritated at being reduced to the role of messenger, when once she'd been so senior. She felt her pain. Used to being in charge of many soul distributions there was no way she was leaving without seeing Val into her new body. Zach might very well be her senior now, but it was his first soul redistribution and any number of things could go wrong.

'Thank you, mother. I'll be there as soon as this soul is safely placed.'

'I don't think so, old girl,' said Zach.

Gabriella sighed. 'Look, Zach. I know you're in charge and I appreciate you want to please the Committee, but it's...'

'No buts, Gabriella. I'm sure I can manage here on my own. You get off and see what they want. Report back to me as soon as you're finished.' He'd been told she could be stubborn and wilful. He would probably have resisted a new boss or mentor in her position too. That's why it was important to stamp his authority at the start. It would be easier for them both if they knew where they stood.

'Are you still here?'

Gabriella knew she'd have to do as told if she wanted to keep her wings. Demoted from grade five to grade three, it had been a long time since she'd had to obey orders from someone of Zach's level.

'You may need my help.' She tried one final time but Zach was having none of it.

'Be gone!'

With a huff and whoosh Gabriella disappeared. Swiftly followed by her mother.

*****

The staff in the labour ward realised something was wrong when their patient screamed in agony. All experienced, they were used to hearing different sorts of screams during labour, but this one signalled trouble. Between exertions she tried to catch a breath to get a few words out.

'Not like this... for the other two. Arrrggggghhhhhh.'

She dug her nails into her husband's hand and he hardly flinched at the pain, too concerned for his wife. This was the third child, a baby girl to complete their family. He'd been present at the birth of both boys and it hadn't been like this. Not at all like this. He wondered if labour was that different depending on the gender of the baby. His thoughts were interrupted by a doctor who told him to get out of the way. His wife had to undergo an emergency caesarean. She was still sleeping from the anaesthetic when the midwife handed the stillborn baby girl to him, wrapped in a blanket. She was like a porcelain baby doll and he cried his heart out as he looked at her perfect face, framed by a shock of black hair.

*****

Val opened her eyes and was surprised to see the light in front of her. She still thought of herself as Val and couldn't move. Her sense of wellbeing vanished as she realised something was wrong.

'Oh dearie me.' Zack said out loud as he pondered what to do next. He was out of his depth but there had to be a solution. Scenes of life on Earth appeared below him. He tried not to panic and, focussing on one, he watched.

An old man was sitting outdoors under a covered area, with a young girl on his lap. Looking straight in front of him he could see the pool, the water rippling from the gentle breeze. He was glad of the breeze, which was a relief from the burning sun.

'Is nanna up in the clouds?' asked the young girl. 'Coz there's no clouds in the sky so where does she go if there's no clouds?'

'Nanna's in the clouds on rainy days but goes back to heaven when the sun is shining,' the man replied.

'Will you live in the clouds with nanna when you die?' asked the child.

'I will, my little Ninja, but hopefully not for a while.' He tickled her and she giggled in delight. She knew it was naughty but Ninja, real name Daisy, didn't miss her nanna because now she could have her granddad all to herself.

Her mother looked out from the kitchen window. It was the first time she had heard her father laugh in the three-month period since her mother's death. It had taken a while to convince him to visit them in Spain and he'd only agreed because her brother was looking after Kale, his beloved Jack Russell. Her thoughts were interrupted as hands encircled her waist and a mouth nuzzled her neck. She turned to face her husband. It didn't take a genius to recognise the meaning of that smile, but she made him ask anyway.

'Millie's at her friend's party and our little Ninja and your father are keeping each other happy. Shall we take a look at the view from the bedroom window?'

She didn't need asking twice. Ben smacked Polly's behind as he rushed up the stairs after her.

Ninja looked up when she heard her grandfather snore. She quietly climbed off his lap and took off her shorts and top. She looked down and smiled. Although she liked fighting at her MMA classes, she wasn't a complete tomboy. Pink was her favourite colour and her bikini was dark pink with swirls of light. Looking at the pool she knew she wasn't allowed in the deep end. It wasn't fair. Millie was allowed to go in the deep end as well as do lots of other stuff that she wasn't. It wouldn't hurt and if she could show her parents she could swim in the deep end she'd be allowed in at other times. She took a run and jumped. Not a strong swimmer, Ninja's head popped above the cold water after she jumped in and she gasped for breath. She paddled about for a bit then decided she'd had enough so paddled towards the side. Seeing a big spider on top of the water she panicked and started splashing about. Forgetting she was in the deep end she tried to stand and swallowed a lot of water before she surfaced. She spluttered and coughed then went under again. This time it took longer for her to break the surface and as she gasped for breath her body felt heavy as she disappeared under the water.

The next time she broke the surface, Ninja tried to call for help but swallowed some of the chlorine tasting water. Her world went into slow motion. Nanna wasn't in the clouds or in heaven because she was smiling and holding her arms open for a cuddle. Ninja didn't want a cuddle from her nanna. She wanted to be back on her granddad's lap cuddling then sleeping. That was a good idea, she'd have a little sleep then tickle granddad again.

Polly dressed and made her way downstairs while Ben was in the bathroom. The house was eerily quiet, so she headed for the kitchen thinking she'd make a dressing for the chicken salad but let Ninja have pizza if she wanted, as Millie had been to a party. She laughed to herself. Ninja was always indignant if one had something the other didn't. Millie said they were having pizzas at the party so Polly knew that's what her youngest daughter would want, even demand, for her tea. If the adults wanted peace this evening, that was the best way forward.

As she looked out of the kitchen window, her brain took a nano-second to register what she saw. Polly ran out of the door screaming. Her father woke from his slumber quickly assessing the situation. He took a run then dived into the water before Polly had reached the end of the pool. Granddad turned Ninja onto her back and dragged her to the side of the pool. Hearing the commotion, Ben ran outside and quickly took in the scene. He wanted to scream but the rational side of his brain, coupled with his training as a former fireman put him straight onto autopilot. His youngest daughter was lying on her back and her mother was leaning over her and so was her grandfather. He took control.

'Polly, call an ambulance, quickly.'

'I think she's gone, Ben, Polly screamed. How could...'

'Go in and call an ambulance, quickly.'

Polly disappeared hoping against hope they could save her. She tried not to think about the consequences if they couldn't.

Ninja watched the scene below her. Somebody who looked like her was lying quietly on the pool tiles and her granddad was leaning over her. Her father told him to move so he could get close and now he was moving her body in different ways. It looked quite rough to Ninja and she didn't like it. Her mother ran into the villa, sobbing, and made a phone call. When she took a closer look she knew she was looking at herself.

'I want to go home,' she shouted and closed her eyes. This must be a dream so when she woke she'd laugh about it and tell Millie what had happened. Ninja opened one eye expecting to be in her bed but she was still up above her body. She started to get annoyed, wanting to be down there and not up here, wherever this was. She had her pizza to look forward to and it wasn't fair if she couldn't have it. She tried to move but was stuck, so all she could do was watch. Fed up at not being able to move, she closed her eyes again to will herself back down to the ground. A whoosh sound made her open them for a look.

A shiny light and a man with wings flew past Ninja and made her spin.

*****

Ben turned his daughter's head but despite the water that had come out of her mouth, her body was still and lifeless. He started CPR, but try as he might there was no response. Polly returned to the poolside after calling an ambulance. She could hear herself wailing but couldn't stop. Her father had his arms around her but she was inconsolable. Ben was determined to get his daughter back and refused to give up. They heard sirens in the background and he kept going with the CPR.

The soul of Val landed and Daisy puked a river of water as she regained consciousness. As she spluttered and coughed, her mother silently thanked God for returning her daughter to them all.

Daisy opened her eyes and looked directly at her mother. *That's not my daughter.* Polly berated herself for the stupid thought, putting it down to the shock of almost losing her. She tried to brush off the weird feeling that Ninja was looking at her through someone else's eye. The next minutes passed in a blur as the paramedics lifted the child and secured her into the back of the ambulance. Her mother accompanied her, watching as they attached wires and needles to various parts of her arms and body. Now awake, her daughter looked terrified and Polly stroked her hair and murmured soothing words.

'You'll be fine, my little Ninja. Everything's going to be all right.'

'My name's Daisy,' she croaked the words, before closing her eyes and falling asleep.

It was the first time she had contradicted anyone for using her nickname and despite the seriousness of the situation, her mother thought it quite peculiar.

*****

Unable to move for the whole performance, Ninja had watched everything from above and was not amused. She tried stamping her feet but nothing happened, then she called out to her parents and granddad but they ignored her. When she saw herself coughing she knew she was still alive, but her seven year old brain couldn't work out why she was watching herself and not living in her body. It was the first time she had had a tantrum where nobody appeared to calm her down, give her what she wanted or tell her to be quiet. When her anger was spent she watched as the ambulance sped to the hospital and her father and granddad followed in the family car. Then the scene below Ninja slowly faded away into darkness. She was very tired and closing her eyes decided to have a sleep, convincing herself that everything would be back to normal when she woke up.

Her version of normal would never be the same again.

Chapter 2

Val's funeral was ten days after her death. It hadn't been a celebration of her life, but a miserable occasion marking her passing and the tragedy her life had become since meeting Big Ed. Predictably it had rained and was still raining now, the day after the funeral. The thunder followed by the rain battering the window and roof woke Tony. He was surprised to see his wife was still asleep. It was the first time since her mother's death that Libby was still sleeping when he'd woken so he knew she must be exhausted. As quietly as he could he grabbed a pair of trackie bottoms, a fleece and put on his slippers. He made his way downstairs, used the bathroom and made himself a coffee.

He sipped his coffee while looking out of the window. The weather appeared to accurately reflect his wife's moods since her mother's death; dark, stormy, sometimes unpredictable and totally depressing. But it was completely understandable and he knew all he could do was to be there for her, to help her ride the storm. Their mother Marion – as a twin he always thought of her as their mother and not his - knew how shocked Libby had been at the way her mother had taken her own life and told him life would never be the same again for any of them. This was proving to be true but Tony knew it was early days and life could only get better. Selfishly, he was looking forward to returning to work the following Monday. Only six days to go and The Director had promised low-level missions where possible during the next few months. If he had to send him away, he would do his utmost to ensure he was home at weekends. *Where possible* were the key words there as Tony knew if something important or urgent kicked off during a mission, not even The Director could guarantee time off. Hell, he couldn't even guarantee they'd keep their lives never mind any holidays.

Tony thought about The School for Personnel with Special Abilities, or SAP as the trained agents liked to call it. It seemed like an age since he was recruited with his twin brother Jim. Although they were now trained agents, The Director and Professor Robert were still interested in their interactions with their dead sister Claire, and how they could be used to prevent both earthly and supernatural crimes. Although he hadn't seen much of Jim since Val's death, they had spoken and communicated telepathically, though it didn't always work. Professor Robert wanted them to develop these skills so he assumed The Director would ask them to focus on this while he needed more time to support Libby, notwithstanding emergencies of course. Thinking of his brother, Tony wanted to speak to him later. Not for anything specific but as a release from the tension and dark atmosphere of the house. He concentrated for a moment, trying to channel his thoughts. He imagined writing a message to Jim, asking what he was up to and telling him he wanted a chat. His mobile phone pinged and before Tony opened it, he knew it was a text from Jim.

'Hang in there bro. Going for a run then back to back meetings. Speak this afternoon?'

Their usual telepathic abilities came to them as naturally as breathing, but the new techniques were absolutely exhausting. Tony was already drained and emotionally weary through looking after Libby, so he wanted to have some energy to get through the rest of the day. Though he suspected Jim already knew that was convenient. He decided to use his phone this time, and replied. *'Great ta.'* He wondered what the meetings were about and if there was a new mission in the offing. Because of his injury before Val's death then compassionate leave since, he'd already been off work far too long. He was itching to get back and fighting that itch with the guilt of leaving his wife. It wasn't all bad. As usual their mother had offered to help. She was away for a few days with her boyfriend but had promised to look after Libby as soon as he returned to work the following week. He knew it was difficult for his mother and for Libby to return to the apartment where her mother had taken her life, but there was no point in putting it on the market so soon after Val's death. Libby had also said that nothing could make her pain

11

any worse and that she wanted him to return to work. Tony thought about their mother again, always amazed at her resilience. She had nursed Val through the final few months of her life, had helped to nurture Melanie the daughter of her ex-husband and their half-sister, and was now readying herself for Libby to move back in for a while so he could swan off back to work. All this after losing one of her own children, their sister Claire. She was an amazing woman and he couldn't wait to meet her boyfriend, just to make sure he was good enough and would look after her in the way she deserved. He had no idea that meeting would come much sooner than expected.

The flush of the upstairs toilet changed Tony's train of thought. He put the coffee machine on and heated the pan. Bacon sandwiches were one of Libby's favourite. She had hardly eaten the day before so he hoped the smell would be enough to tempt her.

She entered the kitchen. Her eyes were swollen and red and his heart went out to her. Tony held open his arms and Libby fell into his embrace. More tears came and he leaned over to switch off the pan as he held her until her crying subsided. She pulled back and shook her head.

'I feel like I'm walking up hill through treacle against a gale force wind. Everything's an effort since mum died and I just want it to stop.'

'It was a shock, Libby. To all of us but especially for you and Carl. It's early days yet, give it time.' He poured her coffee and handed it to her. He suspected she'd never get over the way her mother had died, but now wasn't the time to tell her that.

Libby took a deep drink, hoping the caffeine would reach her bloodstream quickly and give her a burst of energy. If the last eleven days were anything to go by, her hopes would be in vain.

'I'm making us bacon sandwiches for breakfast. Then we're going out to do some shopping. It'll make you feel...' he quickly revised what he was going to say. 'The fresh air will do you good.'

'I'll try to eat the sandwich, but no to the shopping. I'm not ready for that yet.'

Tony thought she was starting to sound exactly like her mother, but quickly wiped that thought from his mind. As much as he loved his wife, he wouldn't be able to cope if she turned into Val. He told himself to get a grip. The woman he loved needed him more than anything just now and all he could think about were his own selfish needs. He forced an air of optimism and put the sandwich down in front of Libby, then refilled her coffee mug.

'Dun ah!' He placed the HP brown sauce next to the sandwich. 'You're not moving until you've eaten all of it.'

His words raised a small smile. 'I'm not five years old you know.'

Tony rubbed her hair as if she was, and Libby smiled again. Maybe everything was going to be all right after all.

He tidied the kitchen as she ate at the breakfast bar.

'Thanks, Tony. I've been thinking you know and maybe it would help if I could talk to mum.'

'And how do you propose to do that?' he asked, already figuring he knew the answer.

'How do you think? You speak to your sister of course to see if she can arrange it.'

Tony tried not to sigh. He thought carefully before choosing his words but had to be straight with her. 'Sweetheart, you know it doesn't work like that. I haven't been able to contact Claire since Val, you know since the day your mother…'

'But that doesn't mean you can't try, does it? And what about Jim?'

He explained that neither had been able to contact Claire. They had no idea she was one of the guardians of evil souls in the cave system known locally as hell on earth.

'Well you'll have to try again. I need to speak to my mother before I can get closure.'

Tony stopped what he was doing then sat opposite Libby holding her hands. 'Do you remember when your father died, Libby and he came to you? Once.'

She nodded and wiped a tear from her cheek. He knew he'd started her off crying again but didn't want to raise any false hopes so had to be completely honest. 'Has he contacted you since then?'

'No, but…'

'Have you spoken to him and tried to summon him?' Tony interrupted.

'Well, yes, especially since mum's died, but he hasn't come back.'

'So you know it's the same for us, sweetheart. We can speak to Claire and call on her, but she will only come to us when she can.'

'But it's not fair, Tony. My dad died the same time as Claire so how can she speak to you two but he can't speak to me. And I'm an orphan now.'

Tony had an image of an Oliver Twist type orphan with a begging bowl asking for more. He couldn't help himself and laughed out loud. His wife totally lost it.

'So you think that me being an orphan is hilarious?' she shouted. 'Well ha, bloody ha ha. I hope you never have to go through what I'm going through at the moment. I ask you to do one thing and all you do is mock…'

'I'm not mocking you, Libby. I'm supporting you the best I know how. I love you. Surely you know that? And I will try to contact Claire. It's just that I don't want to give you false hope.'

'I'm going back to bed, I've got a headache.'

She didn't even acknowledge what he'd said thought Tony as she disappeared up the stairs. 'I'll go and do the shopping,' he said mostly to himself. Roll on next week he thought guiltily.

She lay in bed twisting and turning, unable to go back to sleep. The picture of her mother jumping was an image she would never be able to erase. That, and the thoughts spinning in her head were driving her nuts. Libby

14

dragged herself from bed and took a long, hot shower. She dressed and decided to go for a walk.

A little while later she sat in a coffee shop pondering her future. She felt restless and needed to do something about it. Laughter from another table distracted her. She watched as a woman who looked about the same age as her engaged with the four older people sitting at the table. She gave them leaflets to read and they appeared to hang on her every word. The woman saw her looking and they made eye contact. She smiled and walked over to Libby's table.

'Hi. Now you look like an animal lover. I wonder if I could interest you in our rehoming centre.'

Libby didn't say a word so the woman continued.

'I'm Cassie. Can you spare me some time?'

Libby said she could so the woman sat down opposite her. She outlined what they did at the centre and explained they were looking for new helpers. Libby wasn't big into animals but listened anyway.

'One of our volunteers has retired and the other has just had a baby so it's too much for her. I don't suppose...'

There was something about the woman that fascinated her. She seemed vibrant, exciting and full of life – everything that Libby was not. She wanted to spend time with her in the hope that some of it would rub off.

'I'll certainly come for a look,' said Libby. 'What's a good time for you?'

'How about now?' Cassie smiled. 'I knew you were a dog person.'

They put on their coats and decided to catch the bus to the centre, outside the town. Alighting the bus Libby read the sign arrowed *Glenville Dog Rehoming Centre*.

'It was a farm years ago,' explained Cassie as they walked towards the building a short distance away. 'The last owner was mad about dogs and her daughter agreed to set it up after she died. That was a while ago and it's now well established. The money left by the Glenvilles has long since run out so they used to rely totally on charitable donations, until the current boss took over that is. She's Mrs Glenville's great granddaughter and has moved back recently from the city. She's an entrepreneur,' Cassie rolled her eyes. 'Well that's what she calls herself anyway. As you can see, these buildings are brand new,' she pointed to two modern looking buildings. 'She, Maddie Ross, has started a hotel for dogs where owners can leave their pets when they go away, and also a grooming service.'

'Do you work in both?' asked Libby.

'My job is paid and I'm in charge of marketing and publicity,' she frowned. 'At the moment. But Maddie is overhauling the organisation so watch this space. I help out with the rescue dogs but have nothing to do with the grooming and hotel part of it, except bringing it to the public's attention of course and trying to get some money from them.' She opened the door to the main building and Libby followed her inside. It must have had loads of work done on it since being a farmhouse Libby thought as she looked around. The reception area was bright and modern but not ostentatious. Cassie nodded to the woman at the desk as she passed, then opened another door. There was a concrete pathway and dogs were caged comfortably on each side of the path. Some barked, others were quiet but they all wagged their tails when they saw Cassie.

'Hello you lot,' she said. Cassie stopped to pet a number of dogs, some of them puppies.

'They're adorable,' said Libby, trying to give the three puppies equal attention. She was so enamoured that she didn't notice the woman until she heard her.

'So you've decided to grace us with your presence, Cassie.'

'Hello, Maddie,' said Cassie, deciding to ignore the sarcasm. 'This is Libby, she may be interested in helping out. I said I'd show her around.'

'Hi, Libby, I'm Maddie.' She offered her hand and Libby shook it. 'I do hope you'll be able to spare a few hours each week. We're taking on more and more dogs and need all the help we can get.'

Libby noticed the woman's attitude towards her was totally different than it had been towards Cassie. It was obvious there was no love lost between the two. She already felt an affiliation towards Cassie and took an instant dislike to Maddie.

'Thanks. I'm not sure, but would like a look around if that's okay?'

'Let's go,' said Cassie, not giving Maddie the chance to respond. 'See you later,' she said as they left the boss standing there.

They finished the tour and Cassie waited for Libby's response.

'I want to help out but I'm not sure that cleaning out kennels and feeding lots of dogs is really my thing. Is there anything else I can do?'

'I could always use some help,' said Cassie. 'You know, doing what I was doing when we met.'

Libby thought about it. 'I could try, but I'm not my usual self just now. Something awful happened...' The image of her mother jumping popped into her head and she burst into tears. 'Oh shit, I'm so sorry,' Libby wiped at her eyes. 'You hardly know me and look, I'm a gibbering wreck.'

'It's okay. Whatever it is, you're going to be all right.' Cassie hugged her until the tears subsided. 'Do you want to tell me about it? We can get a coffee if you like?'

'Yes please. Can we walk for a while, I'd prefer that.'

'Of course.'

An hour later they were back at the bus stop and Libby felt better for talking to someone unrelated to her family. Cassie was a good listener and she knew they were going to be friends. They exchanged telephone numbers and agreed to meet up in the town the following week.

As the bus drove away Libby waved to her new friend. Neither knew it was the beginning of a relationship that would change their lives forever.

*****

Marion and Basil were away again. He'd stopped renting the apartment for their time together as Marion had

17

insisted on spoiling him, and it was never much of a break for her. Knowing how stressful her life had been he wanted to take her away from her worries and spoil her instead. This way they could both have fun or rest and recuperate as they wished. This might be their last time away for a while as he was in line for a top position in a government establishment. It was all very James Bond like he thought when he recalled how he'd been approached. It had followed a Thursday clinic at the hospital. As was his custom, Basil popped into the Flying Horse for a drink with his colleagues before catching the train home. He'd been approached by a nondescript woman who called herself Violet. She gave him a card, told him a bit about the job, and asked him to call if he was interested. He called the following day as she knew he would and, after he'd signed the Official Secrets Act, was given further details. Basil had been annoyed about being requested to sign the Official Secrets Act as he abided by the Hippocratic Oath and patient confidentiality. However, after he had signed and she outlined some of the duties, he understood why. He had already taken a number of tests in the South East over a five-day period and had been whittled down to the final three. As he was still only a possible candidate, Basil knew she had only scratched the surface so was intrigued at what else he was to discover. And now it was his final few days with Marion before he had to go off to do some *intensive training and selection* as Violet had worded it. He should have mentioned it to Marion sooner but hadn't wanted to spoil any of their limited time together.

They were walking in the woods adjacent to their countryside hotel, Dordsey Manor, a twenty-minute drive from Marion's home. Wrapped up in scarves and coats to protect them from the blustery autumn winds, the rustling of their feet as they trampled on crisp leaves panicked the wildlife who disappeared before Basil and Marion were anywhere near.

'Penny for them?' said Marion.

'Hmm,' he said squeezing her hand and smiling.

'I know you're distracted so come on, spill. It's obvious you have something on your mind.'

'That transparent eh?'

'Tell me what's bothering you, Basil. Please.'

'It's not bothering me as such. It's just that I've been approached about a new job. It sounds quite interesting and involves what they called intensive training and selection. I'm likely to be out of contact for a few months at least.'

'Ooh, it sounds similar to what my twins were doing. They were head hunted too. Do tell me more.'

'It's assessing the behaviour and suitability of military personnel for certain tasks, my love. I would run the psychiatric department and have a number of staff working for me.' He watched Marion's reaction and she seemed to believe him. He hated lying but there wasn't a lot he could tell her and that was as close to the truth as he understood, from the limited information he'd been given less the psychopaths of course, but he didn't want to worry her so had no intention of telling her that.

'Sounds interesting. I'll miss you of course but I think I'm going to have my hands full with Libby.'

Basil was glad of a change of subject so they discussed what Libby was going through and whether depression could be hereditary. He explained that it often ran in families but there were also triggers that set it off. Since meeting Basil and learning about mental health, Marion was more sympathetic and less inclined to believe that sufferers should get a grip and shake themselves out of depression or dark moods. She was worried for Libby but realised it would take a while for anyone to get over witnessing such a traumatic event, or losing a loved one.

'I'll just have to do my best and care for her the only way I can.'

'But remember to look after yourself too, Marion. Everyone grieves in their own way. If you see symptoms similar to Val, she may need professional help.' He looked up to the sky and felt the first drops of rain on his face. 'Shall we,' he said so they turned around to make their way back to the hotel, knowing exactly what to do to occupy themselves on a wet, English afternoon.

Chapter 3

The Devil was bloody furious. He was still smarting from having to totally destroy some of his best evils who were out of control, but also because of his latest defeat by God. He looked around at the pathetic bunch in front of him, supposedly his top demons. Most were arguing amongst themselves but a few had singled out some lesser evils and were inflicting pain or disgusting acts upon them. These were the ones that interested him. They needed leadership and a few lessons in creativity. He acknowledged they would never have the talents of some he'd had to destroy or those currently in the cave they'd named Hell on Earth. But they could be trained to be disciplined and loyal servants for when the time came. And come it would. The Devil knew the balance of power worked in cycles. Good was currently dominating and he'd never had the patience to wait for the balance to turn. He couldn't sit around doing nothing so he played for a while, inflicting his own suffering on those unfortunate enough to cross his path.

It was hard to be creative when he'd seen and done it all, so he held a council and invited his top demons. He asked for ideas. Afraid of incurring his wrath if they said something out of place, all he received were murmurs and sycophantic responses, making him even madder. Annoyed and impatient, he showed one or two what would happen to idiots who didn't please him.

Different forms of torture followed. One soul was burnt until her flesh melted. She was allowed to heal then endured the same torture over and over. Another had his ears sealed and ants put up his nose; this soul would not come back. As word spread about the horrendous deeds, the top demons worked harder to come up with more imaginative ideas to inflict pain on the weaker.

He selected only those with intelligence and motivation. They were now honed to respond to training and new ideas. The Devil was sure they wouldn't go rogue and disappoint him like Big Ed had, along with Mad Martin.

His next task was to think of a way to pay back God and his goodies for the humiliation he had suffered. Still lacking a sufficient number of talented servants, he knew he couldn't go for full-scale global war on Earth. It would have to be more subtle this time. It hit him suddenly and he wondered why he hadn't thought of it earlier.

*****

They'd kept Daisy in hospital for a few days, not because of any physical injuries, but because her mother said she wasn't acting like her daughter had before the accident. Her mother decided that Millie, Daisy's twelve-year-old sister should visit. They'd told Millie that Daisy had been acting strangely.

'Why are we calling her Daisy all of a sudden?' Millie asked.

Her mother explained that since the accident, Daisy had insisted on being called by her given name. Polly had a flashback to her birth. She was premature and it was touch and go. Her second daughter had to fight for her life as soon as she was born. The medical staff had been kind but honest, preparing the parents for the worst but their girl was a fighter and had proved the experts wrong. As soon as he saw her in the incubator and from his first touch Ben had called her *My Little Ninja* and the name had stuck. She'd loved the name up until she'd almost drowned but now only wanted to be called Daisy.

'I can't get my head around it, mum.'

Polly understood. She couldn't get her head around it either.

'Sometimes people undergo personality changes when they've had a very serious accident,' said Polly. 'We just have to be patient with your sister which will help her to get back to her normal self.'

'Do we want her to be her normal self?' asked Millie and her mother laughed for the first time since the accident, knowing how Ninja, Daisy she corrected herself, could wind up her older sister.

'Come on, let's go and see her.'

22

Daisy was sitting up in bed as they went in and she looked at them suspiciously. Millie had a weird feeling it wasn't her sister in the bed. She looked like her but there was something different that she couldn't quite put her finger on. She felt nervous because of it.

'Hello, Ninja. You had us all worried there.'

'My name's Daisy,' she replied and looked from one to the other. 'Who's she?' the seven year old whispered to the woman who said she was her mother. Millie heard her.

Oh my Lord thought Polly as she saw the colour drain from Millie's face. She did her best to smile at both of her daughters.

'This is your sister Millie. Don't you remember?' The blank look on Daisy's face showed that she didn't.

After an awkward few minutes where Millie told Daisy about significant events in their lives where she'd been happy and a few where she'd had her tantrums, they gave up. When Daisy nodded off to sleep they left.

'I'm frightened, mum. Much as she's a pain I want Ninja back.' Millie bit into her bottom lip, trying not to cry. Her mother hugged her.

'I want her back too. We'll speak to the doctors. I'm sure there's a cure and she'll be all right. It might take time that's all.' Polly wasn't convinced of anything but didn't want to worry Millie any further. None of them could understand it. Daisy had undergone an EEG, MRI a CAT scan and other tests her parents couldn't remember the initials for, and all had been conclusive. There were no obvious signs of brain injury.

For now it was time to go home.

The route from the hospital was a familiar one as they had to pass it to get to the supermarket and shopping mall, which Polly frequented weekly. She always took the girls with her and sometimes they bought new clothes from the mall or a small treat for her daughters before doing the weekly shop in the supermarket next door. Millie and Ninja, - Daisy she corrected herself, she would have to get used to using her daughter's given name so as not to upset her –

found the journey boring and generally played on their iPads. If Daisy was bored or being particularly naughty, she would find some excuse to wind up her older sister and Millie had developed the patience of a saint to deal with her on some days when her mother was driving.

Everything about the journey was different the day they brought Daisy home. Ben had taken the day off from his self-employed building business. They'd decided to throw a bit of a party for her. She was an extrovert and loved parties. Having checked with the medical staff, they believed it might trigger some memories of before the accident and bring her out of herself. Daisy's friends had been invited and a few of the older residents in the estate, to keep her grandfather company. He was almost drowning in guilt. Polly knew that trying to cope with the aftermath of the accident, together with the grief of losing her mother would be too much for him. In any case she blamed herself and Ben for leaving Daisy alone with her grandfather who was already emotional and over-tired.

Daisy didn't play with her iPad. She looked out of the car window and her eyes lit up when she saw the sea.

'I love the sea,' she said shyly.

'Well that's news to me,' said Millie. Saying exactly what her parents were thinking. 'Since when?'

'I don't know, I just do.' Daisy replied almost to herself. 'Can we go there later please?'

A look passed between her parents. They were surprised at her comments, especially as she'd nearly drowned. Polly decided to change the subject. 'Not today, sweetheart we're having a welcome home party for you with all your friends and granddad can't wait to see you.'

'I don't like parties,' Daisy said in a matter of fact voice then went back to looking out of the window.

'What have you done with my real sister?' asked Millie, but her parents didn't laugh. They were wondering the same themselves.

The party confirmed that Daisy was suffering from amnesia caused by the psychological trauma of the accident.

Despite what the doctors had said, Polly was very worried. Her daughter didn't recognise her grandfather or any of her friends. Her extrovert tendencies had also disappeared and she sat on a chair in the corner of the room eating and watching the others without joining in. When Polly phoned the parents of the visiting children and they came to collect them early, she could hardly bear their sympathetic looks. Determined and resourceful, she decided that after a good night's sleep, she would Google Daisy's symptoms then do everything in her power to get her little girl back.

In bed that night she said as much to her husband who agreed wholeheartedly.

*****

Ninja was surprised when nobody came to tell her off when she had tantrums. She wondered when her family were coming to get her and was bored with waiting. She didn't know how long she'd been stuck wherever she was but to her seven year old mind it seemed like an age. Nobody had come to see her since she'd left her body, which wasn't good. Not even her nanna who she had seen when she was in the swimming pool. She wondered if she'd imagined that bit. The only good thing was that she didn't have to go to school. Actually, she wouldn't mind school now because at least she would have someone to talk to.

'Where's my iPad?' she asked aloud. She looked around but this new world was weird. Sometimes there was nothing there and at others it was like a dream. She could see life going on but couldn't do anything about it. Whenever she'd tried to move before she'd been stuck and it annoyed her so she didn't try so often. Unable to resist forever Ninja tried to move again and was surprised to find herself hurtling through the atmosphere. Moving so quickly made her feel sick.

'I want to stop,' she heard herself shouting then hey presto. She suddenly stopped. That made her gag but Ninja was a lot happier. She spent time telling herself to stop and start and laughed like the little girl she was, when it worked like a dream.

'Weeeeeee,' she called out. 'Look at meeccceeee.' But there was nobody about to watch so Ninja decided it was time to go and find someone to join in the fun. She wondered how far away her family were and how long it would take to get back to them.

*****

Zach was worried. He'd checked on young Daisy a number of times and didn't like what he saw. Although the soul of the former Val didn't display signs or memories of her old life, there was no sign of the young girl before the accident. It was as if she had been born again and didn't have any memories. It was a dilemma and worse still was the fact that a seven year old's soul was drifting around the sphere without any love or guidance. If he brought her to Cherussola he would have to admit his mistake but if he left her wandering, she could be susceptible to the influences of any soul that happened to be passing, wherever they were heading. Doing the right thing would mean admitting his mistake and facing the consequences, but Zach wasn't quite ready.

Chapter 4

Tony returned to work but was still worried about his wife. Thankfully, she had moved in with his mother as planned but that didn't stop him from being concerned. It was the Wednesday evening of his second week back in work, and he wasn't due home until Friday. He tried Libby's phone but it went straight to voicemail, so he called his mother.

'Libby's gone out, son.'

Marion explained she was helping out again at the Dog Rehoming Centre. 'I thought she'd told you.'

'No, she hasn't mentioned it. How long has she...'

'I'm not sure, Tony. She said she was going to tell you last weekend, but must have forgotten.'

He was surprised because although Libby liked dogs as much as the next person, she had never shown any particular interest in volunteer work before.

'Is this how she's taking her mind off her mother?' he asked. 'Do you think she's feeling better, mum?'

'Honestly, Tony, I would love to say yes, but she's still nowhere near back to her normal self. Be patient, son and give it time.' Marion didn't add her own concerns about her daughter-in law who had become secretive and started coming and going without telling her. She was an adult and was entitled to do so but was acting so out of character that Marion was worried. They chatted for a few more minutes before Marion said she'd ask Libby to ring him on her return. Libby didn't return his call so Tony didn't speak to his wife until he picked her up from his mother's on the Friday.

'I was worried about you,' he said when they were back in their own place.

'I'm a grown woman, Tony. You don't need to worry about me.'

'Of course I do, it's my job to look after you. And anyway, I thought you might want to talk to me too.'

'I'm going to bed, I've got a headache.' She disappeared up the stairs and he despaired, wondering if he would ever get his wife back. Her personality continued to change and he was in for a surprise later that month.

*****

Basil looked out of the car window, admiring the stunning views of the rolling Welsh countryside. The tests would take place in Wales but the job was in Scotland; it was all very mysterious. He had long given up speaking to Ryan, the man driving the car. He had given the briefest answers to Basil's questions and Basil suspected his role in the organisation was more than driving visitors from A to B. He wondered if the man was quietly assessing him and reporting back his findings. This was disconcerting for Basil, being the one who usually did the assessing.

Shortly after, Ryan stopped the car. They seemed to be in the middle of nowhere, surrounded by lush green hills, but with Army accommodation dotting the landscape.

'We've arrived, Doc. Grab your bag and follow me.'

He did as instructed. As they neared the building Basil looked around. There seemed to be a hive of activity with men and women in different stages of physical training. The instructors looked lean and mean and he felt a small twitch in his stomach. He was at least twenty years older than all the people he could see and if they thought he could even attempt to keep up with them, they could think again.

'Don't worry, Doc, we have different tests depending on job roles and other factors.'

So he was right, Ryan was more than a driver. Not wanting to show he was nervous, Basil decided not to ask Ryan what his physical tests would involve. And anyway, if the journey down was anything to go by, he was unlikely to get a straight answer.

'I'll show you to your accommodation then we'll get some lunch. The work starts later.'

Sounded good so far so Basil followed. He'd had the same work routine for many years and felt a tingle in his stomach. He recognised the excitement mixed with the nervousness. As he looked forward to the unknown, Basil smiled, glad to be out of his comfort zone as he looked forward to the unknown.

*****

Libby enjoyed being around the dog centre, but only because she loved being with Cassie and the puppies who she adored. She liked some of the older dogs but had fallen for the puppies who never failed to make her smile. They would meet at the centre, take the younger dogs for a walk, then she would accompany Cassie on her marketing and promotion efforts. Libby felt she could be somebody else while talking to members of the public and it took her mind off her own worries. She'd grown close to Cassie very quickly. She confided in her like she couldn't with her brother or Tony and his family. Cassie didn't judge and listened as she spoke about the horrors of her mother's death.

'My sister died an horrific death,' Cassie told her matter of factly one day, during their coffee break before heading into the town.

'Christ I'm sorry to hear that,' Libby replied. 'What happened?' Seeing the pain on her friend's face she wished she hadn't been so blunt. 'Sorry, you don't have to tell me if it's too painful.'

'You're right, Libby, it is painful and not something I usually speak about. But I want to tell you, I think you'd understand.' She sighed then got up to close the door. 'She was two years older than me, and the wild child. We had a difficult upbringing. Our uncle, he...I, it's...' She stopped talking and looked down, trying to find the right words. Libby moved to her side and stroked her arm.

Cassie smiled. 'I'm all right thanks, it's just that talking about it brings it all back. But I need to. Anyway, our uncle abused us. Mum caught him trying to rape Kath and went mad. The police were involved. It's not something you ever get over but I seemed to deal with it better than her. She was sexually active at a young age, probably because of what happened, and went all weird. She only dressed in black and decided she was a Goth. She died in her early twenties. A sex game had gone too far and she choked to

29

death. She was with two men. One was done for manslaughter and the other was killed by a truck. They said the bastard was pushed but whatever happened, he deserved it.'

'Oh my God, Cassie. How awful for you and your family.'

'My mother blamed my father coz it was his brother who abused us. Instead of going to prison he disappeared shortly after it all came out and nobody's seen him since. My parents divorced and everything went to ratshit. I went to uni not long after. My mother didn't want me to go at first. She would have wrapped me in cotton wool if she could but I couldn't stand the restrictions at home. I was lucky because they supported me financially. But it's safe to say my family's messed up and we don't have much to do with each other these days. They're both remarried and it sometimes seems like I'm too much a reminder of a past they'd like to forget.' Cassie put a hand over her eyes, trying to stop or hide the tears.

'How awful,' said Libby before enfolding her in a hug. She held her until the tears subsided.

Cassie shook her head and laughed, wiping her eyes with the back of her hand. 'Look at me, crying like a schoolgirl for God's sake. Right. Now you know my life story and I know all about you. We're bruised, Libby but we're survivors you and I. Whatever life chucks at us we can just tell it to sod off, as long as we've got each other.'

'Spot on,' said Libby, knowing the woman now standing in front of her was a friend for life.

'Shall we make a move?'

Libby smiled her agreement looking forward to a change of scenery after the emotional twenty minutes they'd just endured.

*****

As he ate his lunch, Basil was relieved to see six other middle-aged people arrive, all at different times. Like him they were dressed in Army issue kit but wearing their own boots. They'd been briefed to break-in sturdy boots prior to arrival. He wondered what roles they were being considered for. The introductions commenced and he assumed their names were nicknames, or pseudonyms, just like his.

'This is Bazzer,' Ryan said as each new arrival took their place. Basil tried to hide his amusement at the nickname; he had never been called Bazzer in his entire life. There were now eight of them at the table, with spaces for two more. He was surprised to see identical twins walking towards the table. There was something familiar about them so he checked his memory. No, he definitely hadn't met them. People often had mannerisms or personality traits similar to others so he wondered who they reminded him of. He parked the thought to one side knowing he had more important matters to deal with today. It would come to him in due course.

'This is J and T,' said Ryan. 'They're here to mentor you and to assess your abilities. We'll go to the briefing room after lunch where you'll hear about what delights we have in store for you during the next few days.' They all smiled nervously except for Basil. He was thinking of discussions he'd had with Marion when she'd told him about her twins, Anthony and James. She'd said they both worked in some sort of high-powered jobs for Arbuthnot and Lee, one of the FTSE top one hundred companies in the UK. He looked at the twins and figured he was letting his imagination run riot. It was all this cloak and dagger stuff. Basil silently vowed to get a grip and deal with the facts, not supposition.

The physical tests were harder than expected so Basil was glad he'd trained hard on the run-up to his arrival. He really wanted this job and had already sussed the two other applicants for the head psychiatrist post. He realised they were likely sussing him out too. Out of the seven who had started the programme, Basil was one of the four remaining after spending a full day marching then overnighting in a tent on the Brecon Beacons. The good news was two men and one woman had left voluntarily, or been told to leave – he wasn't sure which – but he was certain that one of the men had been in the running for the

31

same post as he was. So it was down to him and the other woman. Unfortunately she seemed more than capable.

The physical tests over, the twins said their goodbyes and disappeared. The next tests involved Command Tasks where their leadership and teamwork was tested, together with various diagnostic tests and grillings in front of a panel where they were given scenarios and had to explain what they would do and why. To Basil the mental tests were more draining than the physical and he was almost glad when he was called in front of a team to be interviewed. This was not an unpleasant experience like the other tests, but he sensed the underlying toughness of the man who led the interview panel, though he was charming, charismatic, looking and acting like the director of a corporate business.

When it was over they said goodbye then went their separate ways, all in different cars. Basil was with Ryan. Having already figured that Ryan was a big cheese within the organisation, he wondered whether the importance of his driver signified success or otherwise. There was no point questioning Ryan. He had done everything he could and knew he'd tried his best. When he'd applied for the post Basil wanted a change but wouldn't have been too disappointed had he not been selected. He corrected himself, he was competitive so his ego would have taken a blow, but not much else. Something had changed. He'd felt a new lease of life and really wanted this job. He could only hope he was a better applicant than the woman who was as fit as him, had good leadership skills and was bubbly and friendly, as well as kind and good-looking. *Damn*, he thought, doubting his own abilities for the first time in years. Knowing only misery could come out of this thought process, he forced his thoughts elsewhere. It was Thursday afternoon and he wasn't due back to work until the following Monday. Tomorrow would be spent on the practicalities of washing his dirty clothes and doing his homework on the cases for the following week. The lady who helped with his housework and washing, and made him the occasional home-cooked meal, didn't come in until Monday. There was no way he could leave his dirty washing, mostly soiled by the wet Welsh countryside, until then. He was looking forward to seeing Marion and meeting her sons and their wives at dinner on Saturday night. They'd decided to do it one at a time so she would meet his daughters later. Much later for his oldest as she now lived in Australia and Basil only saw her once a year. He hoped to take Marion on the next visit but hadn't yet broached the subject.

Saturday evening soon came around and he felt a bit like a teenager meeting his girlfriend's father for the first time. He gave himself a quick visual check over before knocking Marion's front door.

Tony jumped up to answer it.

'I'll get it,' said Fiona. The twins and Libby left her to it, knowing she was the nosiest in the group. But Marion put her straight.

'It's okay thanks, Fi. I've got it.' Fiona sat back down next to Libby. They were all quiet, trying to listen to the greeting.

'Hello,' whispered Marion, knowing exactly what her sons and their wives were like. She kissed Basil on the lips then he handed over the flowers. 'Oh they're lovely, Basil. Thank you so much.'

'Beautiful flowers for a beautiful lady,' he whispered and all the others could hear was Marion's giggles.

'She sounds like a schoolgirl for Christ's sake,' said Tony. His wife had that faraway look in her eyes and ignored him.

They looked to the door as it opened. 'Baz...' said Jim before trying to hide it with a weird sounding cough. He got up to go to the kitchen, saying water in between coughs.

Basil could see why he was surprised. So he wasn't the only one misleading Marion.

'Well aren't you going to do the introductions, Tony? Asked Marion. It was unlike her twins to be so rude.

'Sorry, mum. Jim's coughing fit threw me a bit.'

'Hello, Basil. I'm Tony and this is my wife Libby. This is Fiona and...'

'and I'm Jim,' said Jim. 'Something stuck in my throat earlier. 'Pleased to meet you at long last. What line of business are you in again?' he asked with a knowing twinkle in his eyes.

'Give me a chance to take Basil's coat before you grill him,' said Marion. 'Come on, Tony, chop chop, you haven't even offered the poor man a drink yet.'

Now it was Basil's turn to be amused. If he'd had any doubts before, he now knew exactly who was boss in this family.

Chapter 5

The novelty of being a bat and watching the evils suffer had long since worn off. Claire, Raphael, Ron and Sandy knew their shifts as demon guards were nearly over. The others would stay to train up the new guards so Claire believed she and Raphael would be called back first, followed by Ron and Sandy. Her assumption was correct and as soon as she heard the whoosh, she knew it was a messenger. She was surprised to see it was Gabriella who she considered far too senior for the role. Gabriella explained about her demotion and Zach's promotion.

'I also need to speak to you about a few other matters but will do so when we reach home and can talk in private.'

As intrinsically curious as she was, Claire knew better than to probe Gabriella for further information. It would be a waste of time so she'd just have to wait. After briefing the guards who were replacing her and Raphael, they said goodbye to Ron and Sandy.

'Won't be long before you're back with us and in your proper spirit body.'

Ron said a quick goodbye but didn't stay to watch them leave. Claire was relieved and knew Ron was desperate to leave too. She didn't want to linger; it would be like rubbing salt in his wounds.

As soon as they left the cave they were caught up in a swirl of air. Both closed their eyes and didn't attempt to talk. They would have been fighting the noise and it wasn't worth it. The swirl disappeared. Claire and Raphael found themselves holding hands. He touched one of her wings and she shivered in delight, thrilled to be back in her angel form and anticipating the pleasures of the angel she loved when they arrived at Cherussola. Gabriella could sense where this was heading and coughed, breaking the spell between the lovers.

'Plenty of time for that later,' she tried not to laugh when Claire blushed. 'Welcome back.'

Raphael gave her a winning smile and without further words they headed for home.

*****

Ron and Sandy, along with the other guards, watched them leave, envious of their freedom but knowing their turn wasn't far away. All was quiet in the cave as they went about their duties, checking the inmates and ensuring there were no escape routes. He looked at the roaches as he flew. It was impossible to keep a count of the exact number of evils, there were too many of them, but their minders had a rough idea and were satisfied there were no gaps in the many hidden nooks and crannies of the deep and dark cave system. He felt a change in atmosphere as he flew. Others felt it too as the bats screamed to warn each of their colleagues. Ron landed as soon as he could and watched as for the first time ever, all the cave's creatures stopped what they were doing. Massive shudders shook the area and some of the bats flew near to the cave's entrance so they could see outside. Looking up at the cliff face, they could see that the earthquake had caused rocks to fall and one side of the cliff was now a lot higher than the other. A crack appeared down the higher side of the cliff and the solid stone began to fall off in chunks. The rumble became louder and louder as the rocks headed towards the cave. The bats moved inside and waited for the rocks to hit. The sound was overpowering as the avalanche of stone tumbled towards the cave and the impact was deafening. The cave shook and some of the guardians lost their balance. One landed on the floor and the cockroaches were all over him like a tramp on chips. The bat screamed in agony as they wasted no time in tearing him to bits. The other bats screeched as they flew at the roaches, doing their best to pull them off. A light appeared then disappeared out of the now small cave entrance. At least the guardian's soul had managed to escape. There was little remaining of the bat's body as the roaches fought over the sweet meat of their former guard.

A number of roaches hadn't joined the melee. They knew the bats were distracted and had been waiting for this opportunity since arrival. By the time the bats saw the cockroaches heading for the fissure that had been caused by the earthquake, it was too late to catch the escapees. Ron quickly moved to the gap along with a number of other guardians, in order to prevent further escapes. The dark souls were furious, knowing it could be an eternity before they had another opportunity. As they watched a number of dark orbs disappear into the atmosphere, they didn't wish them well. Such was the nature of the dark souls, they hoped the former cockroaches would eventually end up as slaves of their master in Hell and undergo an eternity of pain and degradation.

*****

The dark souls went their separate ways, most happy to enjoy the feeling of freedom without making any future plans. Two of them stayed together.

'I'm free, I'm free,' shouted Goth. 'And I've got a list of those I'm going to payback. Big style.'

Harry laughed. Basking in the delight of being back in his teenage body and revelling in the smell of sweet air. He would never forget the rancid stench of thousands, possibly millions of cockroaches and never wanted to be anywhere near that place again. If only the locals knew how accurate their description of *infierno terrenal* was. It was literally *Hell on Earth* as far as he was concerned.

*****

As they arrived in Cherussola Gabriella looked at her brother and the soul who filled his world. They only had eyes for each other and she didn't need to be a genius to see what they were thinking. She decided to at least try to get their attention.

'Welcome back. There have been some changes we need to discuss.'

They were totally absorbed in one another and ignored Gabriella, until she clapped her hands loudly.

'Why don't you two get settled in and rest. Then we'll get together later.'

37

They smiled, said their goodbyes then hurried to their home.

Claire concentrated, imagining a secluded beach where the sun was shining but a cool breeze stopped them from burning. The sea was almost tideless so they could hear a gentle lapping in the background, along with the sweet song of a rare bird. A king-sized bed was in the middle of their beach and they made their way to it, hand in hand. They made love over and over then slept and when they awoke they made love again. There was no need for words, they communicated their love by look and touch. After satisfying each other and letting sleep refresh their minds, they knew it was time to return to work.

'Shall we?' asked Rafael.

'Much as I'd love to stay in this bubble forever, I believe we have to fight the fight,' Claire sighed. 'Is it ever over?'

'No, my love. All we can hope is for the balance of peace and kindness to outweigh that of chaos and evil. The lulls are generally followed by the storms.'

'Let's go and see what Gabriella wants to talk to us about. I want to check in with my brothers as soon as I can too.'

They held hands and whizzed off to find Gabriella.

She'd been waiting patiently. 'Ah, the lovers arrive at long last. I assumed you'd returned to the cave.'

Claire was about to respond but Raphael gave her a look, telling her not to rise to the bait. She put on her most angelic face. 'We're well rested now, Gabriella, thanks for your patience. How can we help?'

Touche thought Gabriella. She gave them a big smile; it was good to have them back.

'You know I was demoted to Grade Three and Zach promoted?' they nodded so she continued. 'I had to work for Zach and was there to watch his first soul redistribution shortly after you left.

'Val?' asked Claire and Gabriella nodded.

38

'As he was about to transport her, our mother turned up,' she looked at Raphael. 'to tell me the Committee wanted to see me. I didn't want to leave Zach in case something went wrong and told him as much. He disagreed and told me to leave immediately.'

'Kind, thoughtful Zach said that? And your mother's a messenger too? That's ridiculous.'

'Yes to both,' said Gabriella. 'It seems that Zach knows how determined I can be so decided to rule with an iron fist so to speak.'

'Either that or the power has gone to his head,' said Raphael.

'Whatever the reason, I was as surprised as you both. Much as I wanted to disobey I couldn't risk being in more trouble with the Committee and facing another possible demotion. If that happened I would have to take orders from newly promoted angels and that just wouldn't work. The same could have happened to our mother, Raphael if I didn't report to the Committee as quickly as I could, so you can see my dilemma.

Even though she was a relatively new angel herself, Claire was inclined to agree with Gabriella's decision.

'So what happened?'

'I'm coming to that, Claire. The baby that Val's soul was meant for died before Zach got to her, so he had to find a new host. Instead of Val being in the holding area while Zach found a new host, he decided to put her in the body of a seven year old.'

'So both souls are in the new host body?' asked Raphael, knowing what problems this could cause. There were people walking the streets and in institutions who spent their time arguing with the voices in their heads. Not all of them had received the correct diagnosis and some were victims of double-soul errors. The angels worked hard to ensure this didn't happen, but sometimes made mistakes. When they did, they worked their hardest to rectify them when they were brought to their attention.

'No they're not,' his sister's voice brought him back to the present. 'Val is now Daisy and the former Daisy must be somewhere between Earth and Cherussola. At least that's what I hope. At seven years old I'd like to think she hasn't been pulled to the other side'.

'So what has Zach said about this?'

'Therein lies the problem, Claire. Zach hasn't come clean. I assume he doesn't want me to know he's made a mistake.'

'In the meantime this child soul could be susceptible to anyone who happens to run into her?' asked Raphael, but he already knew the answer.

'Exactly.'

'Do we tell the Committee?'

'No point, Claire,' said Gabriella. 'The Committee would allocate angels to find Daisy's lost soul then probably send her to heaven. If we manage to find her, we might be able to put her parents and loved ones out of their misery.'

'You mean we could take…'

'Let's say no more about it now, Claire and cross that bridge when we come to it.'

Claire was happy to have a mission but there was something else she needed to do first. 'Is there time to see how my brothers are getting on first?'

'Of course. She's been in the ether for six months now in Earth time so a little while longer shouldn't make a difference. Besides, the worst evils are contained in the cave so she should be relatively safe until we discover where she's hiding. That's if we are able to find her of course.'

Gabriella had no idea how wrong she was.

Chapter 6

Jim and Tony were on surveillance, responding to information that a child was being used as a drug runner. Nothing unusual about that unfortunately, but what was unusual was the eleven year old had been a model child up to a few weeks earlier. She was from a good home where her parents worked hard and didn't pander to her every desire. Her older brother was a normal teenager, if there was such a thing thought Jim, and Louisa had loved ponies and playing the saxophone. Her mother was Head Teacher in a primary school and her father the head of the advertising department in a top five hundred company. Both were worried about Louisa's complete personality change, or that's how it seemed to them and Louisa's brother. The twins were bored so Tony decided to share his worries about Libby.

Jim spoke before Tony explained.

'How is she?'

'Still the same.'

'Is her work helping?'

'She decided she couldn't concentrate on her job while grieving for her mother so she's given it up. But she's helping out at a dog rehoming centre.'

'Dog rehoming? That's good I suppose but she was so excited about that job. What about...'

'Exactly what I said,' Tony shook his head. 'There was not point trying to talk her out of it. She said she couldn't do anything until we made contact with Claire to find out what's happening with her mother.'

'Did somebody mention my name?'

The twins were surprised. They hadn't sensed Claire's presence so she must have just arrived. Before being trained for their current role they would have jumped at the suddenness of her arrival, but not now.

'Welcome back, sis,' said Jim. 'Where have you been?'

If she hadn't been able to see the smiles on their faces, she would have heard it in Jim's voice. She was so

41

grateful to still be in touch with her brothers. They had a strong and unusual bond when she was alive and it was still there, now that she was dead.

'That's not important. I'm back now and that's what counts.'

Knowing it was code for *I can't tell you* there was no point in pushing her. 'Any reason for this particular visit?' asked Tony.

'I wanted to catch up with you and hear what you've been up to. And how's Libby?'

So she hadn't heard the earlier conversation, thought Tony. He explained Libby had left her job. 'I'm really worried, Claire. She seems to be turning into her mother in front of my very eyes and nothing I do seems to help. I took some time off work but mum said she was even worse when I was at home so I'm back.'

So her mother was looking after Libby as she did Val, what a saint. She'd speak to the twins about her mother later but wanted to see if she could do anything to help the Libby situation. Claire saw the look between her brothers and knew they hadn't told her something.

'What is it?'

'Libby insisted I contact you to ask where her mother is and if she's okay. She says it's the only way she can get closure.'

'Hmm. What did you tell her?'

'I did my best to contact you, Claire but you were obviously otherwise engaged.'

He sounded disappointed. Claire adored her brothers and would do anything she could for them, but there were certain matters she could not discuss on orders from the Committee. Frustrating as it was, she knew her powers might be removed if she broke too many rules and she could be moved on, unable to visit her brothers ever again.

'If I don't come when you need me, it's because I'm helping someone else. I'm sorry but that's just the way it is.'

'So you're not in charge of your own destiny?' asked Jim.

'Is anybody?'

Tony changed the subject. 'So is there anything I can tell Libby about her mum, Claire?'

'I don't see every soul that passes, Tony. Just because there's a family connection, it doesn't mean I know what's happened to Val.' She chose her next words carefully. 'You can tell Libby I'm sorry but there's nothing I can tell her about her mother.'

'You were my only hope, Claire,' said Tony, clearly distressed. 'Now I have to watch my wife's state of mind deteriorate even more, knowing there's absolutely nothing I can do for her.'

'I didn't say there was nothing I could do. I may be able to help but will have to check a few things out first. I don't want to raise your hopes but can you find out what items of Libby's or her mother's gave them a particular connection? Then next time I'll see what I can do.'

'I don't need to check. There's a photo of Libby and her mother before Val became ill. Libby keeps it on the bedside table, on her side of the bed. There's also a lilac coloured scarf thing that Val often wore when she was in bed. It certainly wasn't to keep her warm as it's really thin and wispy. Libby often holds that to her and sniffs it. It must remind her of her mother.'

'That's enough to go on. Okay I'll get right to work, but before I go, how's mum?' Claire wouldn't have the time to look in on her mother so hoped she wasn't under too much strain.

'Besides for the situation with Libby, she seems happy.'

'That's an understatement,' said Jim. 'I think she's serious about this new man.'

It was wonderful for Claire to hear this news. After the grief her father had given her mother then the stress of her volunteer work abroad, meeting one of the most evil people ever and looking after Val, and helping with Melanie, her mother needed something for herself. Claire vowed to look in on both of her parents when time allowed. But for now, the Libby situation was the priority and she hoped Gabriella would give her permission to try to make life better for her sister in law.

'I'm so glad mum's found happiness at last. I have to go now but will be in touch as soon as I can.'

Claire disappeared. In her haste to find a way to help Libby, she didn't think to ask them about their mission and would have been concerned if she knew what they were doing.

The boys didn't hear the whoosh but already knew their sister was no longer with them.

*****

'I need to ask Gabriella a favour.' Claire said to Raphael back in Cherussola.

'She's kind of busy, Claire. She said Ron and Sandy were returning shortly and the Committee had told her it was time for Ron to make a decision.'

They both knew what that meant. Selfishly, Claire hoped that Ron would decide to stay.

'And there's something else too.'

Claire gave him a look and he continued.

'Apparently we can't be trusted to work on our own without getting into trouble so we are to have mentors.'

'But Gabriella's my mentor,' said Claire. 'And you of course she added hastily,' before giving him a kiss to smooth the waters.

'We can't act as mentors because of our demotions. Martin is going to mentor me but I haven't been told the name of yours.'

Claire knew it was imperative for her to speak to Gabriella before her mentor was assigned. Otherwise she would never be able to help Libby. Asking permission was now out of the question and she didn't want Raphael to know her plans. Claire would suffer the consequences if there were any, but there was no way she was going to drag anyone down with her, especially the angel she loved.

'Before I do anything I need to see how my family are getting on. My mum's been under a lot of pressure lately and it seems like an age since I've visited my father and step-sister.'

'But can't that wait?' asked Raphael. 'The Committee have summoned us both, Claire, and you don't want to try their patience, especially as we're on a sticky wicket already.'

'I'm really sorry, Raphael but no, it can't wait.'

He looked deep into her eyes as if probing her very being. Claire looked away knowing her game was up. She was in a no win situation; either do what she must with the chance she'd get into trouble and drag Raphael down with her, or leave well alone and risk Libby going the same way as Val. As she started crying she'd made up her mind and whatever Raphael wanted to do was his own decision.

'Whatever it is I'm coming with you. We can face the consequences together.'

It was as if he'd read her mind so she hugged him fiercely, feeling much stronger for his comfort and support.

Eventually she composed herself and unhugged her beautiful angel. 'Come on let's go. I'll explain on the way.'

*****

The twins prepared themselves for movement not long after Claire had left. They were ready for it as the house was bugged and they'd heard the argument.

'I'm going out and you can't effing stop me.'

'Louisa! Do not use that foul language.' Her mother didn't shout but was firm.

'Effing, effing, effing,' she shouted and both parents looked on in shock as she left the house, slamming the front door behind her.

The twins informed their street team who started following Louisa. The followers changed every now and then so the girl wouldn't get suspicious. She stopped at a bus stop and smoked a cigarette as she waited, which the twins knew would shock her parents. Getting onto the bus, Louisa got off at the Brightside Council Estate – there was some irony in the name as it was a dark and gloomy place and a haven for the criminal classes.

She chatted to two men before one handed Louisa a package. She took it and hood up, head down, made her way towards a block of flats. The follower passed the block as Louisa entered; they would now have to rely on the bug hidden in her favourite hoody. She made two exchanges before exiting the building a few minutes later. She went into three more buildings doing a few deals in each one. The twins and street team assumed the deals were completed when Louisa left the last building then headed back towards the bus stop. Instead of carrying on walking along the main road, she took a left and walked up a back lane.

Assuming she was to meet the men who gave her the drugs, the twins left their car and quickly made their way to the other end of the lane, hoping to take some discreet photographs of the youngster and the two men they assumed, had convinced Louisa to act as their mole. Hiding behind a skip, they were able to see without being seen and could hear the conversation through the bug in Louisa's top. There was enough background noise from some of the back yards for Tony to remove his phone from his pocket and press the record button. The conversation wouldn't be clear but they'd have something concrete to show the professor and other staff at the school.

'Give me all the fuckin' money, kid.' The taller of the men said to Louisa.

'If you think I'm taking all the risks for the fucking crap you're paying me, you can think again,' said Louisa.

The twins exchanged a surprised look. 'She thinks she's a gangster's moll or something,' said Jim and Tony shushed him.

The second man ignored Louisa and spoke to the taller one. 'This one's getting too big for her boots, mate. Bout time we taught her a lesson.' He leered at Louisa then grabbed his crutch and made an obscene gesture.

'Oh you fucking think so do you?'

46

The twins watched in amazement as the eleven year old took a flick knife out of her pocket, opened it, and without hesitation, stabbed the shorter man in the stomach. He doubled over in agony then collapsed to the ground. A look of utter surprise on his face.

'Want some of this, Rav,' she asked the taller man as the twins rushed from their hiding place and ran to the scene. The man she'd called Rav legged it in the opposite direction. The twins weren't concerned, knowing he would be apprehended by their team. Louisa turned to them, making jabbing actions with the knife.

'And who the fuck are you?' she asked.

'Drop the knife,' said Tony.

Louisa had no intention of dropping the knife.

Tony raised his hands in the air and started to clap.

'What the fuck?' said the charming young lady, looking at Tony's hands.

The distraction worked as Jim approached her from behind. He grabbed her wrist and twisted. Louisa dropped the knife and screamed in pain. Furious, she started kicking out and shouting obscenities that would make most grown men blush. She was still screaming as the paramedics arrived to treat the wounded man, followed by the police. The officers had to tie her hands and legs. Still mad, Louisa bit one so they put her against the wall until the caged van arrived to take her away.

'All in a day's work,' said Jim as they watched the vehicle leave. Neither smiled at his comment.

*****

As much as she'd tried, Ninja couldn't get back to her own family. Still nobody came when she cried or had tantrums so she had to keep herself amused which wasn't easy, as there was nothing to do. She didn't even have an iPad. Then one day when she opened her eyes she saw a scene below her. It was the first time she'd seen anything except the space around her and lights passing to and fro, and she was fascinated. A grown up woman was walking across the road, laughing to herself as she played with her

47

phone. She didn't see the car as it sped right into her and Ninja screamed when she saw the woman smash up against the windscreen before her body flew over the car then came to rest on the road behind it. She screamed again when the car behind tried to swerve to avoid the woman but drove straight into her. The drivers of both cars ran to where the woman lay but they were shaking their heads and Ninja thought they looked upset. She saw a light leave the woman's chest, move up above her and hover for a while. She didn't know how long the light stayed there before it moved up to the sky. Later, the woman who had been knocked over came near to Ninja.

'Hello,' she said but the woman ignored her and passed her by shortly after. She watched as the woman got smaller then disappeared from sight. She had only seen bright or dark lights pass her before and this was the first time she'd actually seen a person. Her seven year old mind tried to process the scene as she looked back down at the woman lying in the road. An ambulance had now arrived and one of the car drivers was crying. The woman was put on a stretcher and covered with a blanket. When they covered her face Ninja understood she had died. She now thought that she might actually be dead. *But if I'm dead, why hasn't nanna been to see me,* she asked herself. After spending some time thinking about it, she wondered if it was because she liked her granddad the best and her nanna had guessed.

From that time on Ninja saw people rather than lights. Desperate for company, she tried to talk to everyone she saw but they always seemed to be heading somewhere in a hurry. Some didn't see her but those she knew had seen her, didn't even say hello. Her parents had told her that good manners were very important so she was surprised at the number of people who were being so rude. It was less boring when she could watch events happening below her, some were like the grown-up films she'd sneakily watched from the top of the stairs when her parents thought she was sleeping. Others were just people going about their day-to-day lives.

Some of the scenes Ninja would have found totally boring when alive, were now fascinating.

Two people came at her out of nowhere. Ninja didn't have time to move out of their way and knew they were going to crash right into her. She screamed. Nothing happened and when she heard laughter she risked opening one eye. They had stopped right in front of her

'Well hello, little girl.'

It was the boy who spoke. He was dressed in clothes from old black and white films and had a funny haircut.

'Hello,' Ninja replied.

'What are you doing here?' asked the woman.

Her face was very white and she wore black clothes, make-up and nail varnish. Even her lips were black. It reminded Ninja of some Halloween costumes and she wondered if she was going to a party.

'Is it Halloween,' she asked.

The boy looked at his companion and laughed. 'Cheeky sod,' the woman said as she gave him a quick kick. The boy shouted in surprise and went hurtling through space. They both watched as he managed to stop himself and made his way back to them.

'That wasn't very nice,' said Ninja.

'I don't suppose it was. What's your name?'

'It's Daisy but everyone calls me Ninja.'

'Well that's a really cool name. I'm Goth and this one here is Harry. What are you doing here, Ninja?'

'I think I'm dead. I'm bored and I miss my mummy and daddy. And I miss Millie.'

'Do you want to have some fun?' asked Goth as she held out a hand.

She'd been on her own for too long and was desperate to do something and have new friends. They were a lot older but that didn't bother her. 'Yes please,' she said as she took Goth's hand and they went flying through the ether.

Ninja had no idea where they were going and she didn't care.

*****

Claire didn't have time to visit any other family members except Libby, but it would be a bonus if her mother was at home. Her plan was to go in, do the job then return to Cherussola. She would need to rest before seeing the Committee as moving anything physical could be draining, especially as she'd been a bat for a while and was out of practice. She'd explained her plan to Raphael and he had offered to help. He would be in as much trouble as Claire for going with her and not trying to stop her, so had declared *in for a penny in for a pound*. They arrived at her mum's apartment but nobody was there. So Tony must be home this weekend she thought, so they headed to his house.

Tony was downstairs preparing dinner. A football match was on the TV and he was going back and forth from the kitchen to the living room every time he heard the crowd roar or the commentator becoming excited. They floated upstairs. Libby was lying on the bed, facing the window. It seemed she was looking out but Claire thought she looked miles away. The thin lilac scarf was on the back of a chair. Here goes thought Claire as she started to concentrate. It was her first attempt at moving anything since being transformed back to angel. It would normally be an easy task but she was out of practice. It worked at the second attempt as the scarf started to move.

Libby was so deep in thought that it took a few seconds for her to realise the scarf was moving. She sat up on the bed and watched in fascination as the scarf was placed gently over her shoulders.

'Mum, mum? Is that you, mum?'

Although she hoped it was her mother, it was still pretty scary. Libby started shaking then threw a hand to her mouth to stop herself from screaming. She tried to get a grip. Wasn't this what she'd wanted since her mother died. She sniffed the scarf, convincing herself it had a stronger aroma of her mother's perfume.

'Oh, mum,' she said. 'Are you all right? Are you with dad now?'

In answer the photograph of Libby and her mother moved from the bedside table and was placed onto the bed next to Libby. Claire mouthed a silent thank you to Raphael who had made it look effortless. Libby picked up the photo and hugged it to her chest, then felt a hand stroke her hair. It seemed weird because her mother hadn't been very tactile when living. She must want me to know she loves and misses me, thought Libby. And she did feel loved, like she never had before. The thoughts that had tormented her since her mother's death disappeared, and Libby felt a calm that had evaded her for six months. She closed her eyes and slept peacefully for the first time in ages.

Raphael and Claire smiled at each other. Being an angel wasn't all hard work and it was wonderful to see the rewards of their love and compassion. Claire decided to have a quick word with Tony. He sensed her presence straight away.

'It's done,' she said. 'I have to go.'

She heard his quick thanks before joining Raphael to make their way back. They would need to be on their best form in front of the Committee, so although feeling less drained than they expected, they would need a rest first to recharge their batteries before appearing before them.

*****

Tony knew if he left her sleeping, Libby would be awake during the early hours of the morning and getting through the following day would be a struggle for her. The curry was simmering gently and the rich smell filled the rooms downstairs. He could still smell it as he made his way upstairs and was surprised it hadn't woken her. It would have before her mother died. Tony was eager to see the results of Claire's intervention, but knew he had to hide his excitement so Libby wouldn't suspect. He hated deceiving his wife but if it meant she would be happier, then the end justified the means.

'Libby,' he leaned over her. 'You need to wake up, sweetheart, otherwise you won't sleep properly tonight.'

She opened her eyes smiled at him then stretched lazily. He thought straight away the old Libby was back.

'I've had a visit, Tony. Mum's been so she must be all right.'

'Oh wow! That's fantastic. What happened?' Tony sat on the bed next to her and listened as she outlined her experience.

'The feelings of walking up hill through treacle since she died, have disappeared. It's as if I've turned a corner and can look forward to things again,' she wiped away a lone tear. 'I'm so sorry for what I've put you through, Tony.'

'Don't be silly. Grief affects us all differently. I remember when Claire died...'

It had been awful for the twins. They had been devastated by their sister's death but there was some relief when they knew they could still have a relationship with her, albeit an unusual spirit-type relationship.

Libby held his hand, silently comforting. Tony silently thanked his sister for returning his wife to him.

His body did the thinking for him and he rushed to strip off like there was no tomorrow. Libby hadn't felt like making love since her mother's death and though he knew he had to be patient, Tony was desperate to have some intimacy with his wife.

He'd barely satisfied his needs, knowing Libby was simply going through the motions. He dressed while she was in the shower and wondered again whether his wife would ever return to her former self.

Chapter 7

'Where are they?' asked the recently promoted Angelo. The Committee were tired of waiting and were becoming impatient. They all looked at Zach.

'I'm sorry for their tardiness, I'll have words,' he said.

'I asked you where they are,' Angelo repeated leaning forward this time for emphasis.

'I'm not... I'll go and find out and bring them to you,' Zach replied.

There were rumblings and some whispers amongst the Committee members.

'Find them but don't bother bringing them to us yet,' said Angelo. 'We've already made our decision.'

'May I ask what that decision is?'

'All in good time, Zach.'

Gabriella and Amanda had heard every word and knew the best they could hope was for Raphael and Claire to be demoted. The worst would be to lose their wings and be sent beyond eternity to heaven. Most would be ecstatic, but not Raphael and Claire who enjoyed being working angels, fighting the never-ending war against evil and helping good, but tormented souls when they could. The fact that Claire was still in touch with her brothers was also a privilege enjoyed by few.

They would have to do something very special to lessen the wrath of the Committee. Neither Gabriella nor Amanda could see that happening any time soon.

*****

It was always good to have another servant, thought Goth, as she decided to recruit Ninja to her cause. She knew she'd have to groom her and wouldn't take her to visit her family yet for two reasons. The child wasn't strong enough to do what Goth planned and she didn't want to upset her. She asked for the name of Ninja's school and soon enough they were hovering over her classroom.

'Who's your best friend?'

'Kelly Gilbert there,' she pointed to the girl with the long ginger hair. 'Her birthday's on the same day as mine and last year we had two parties...'

They let her ramble on for a bit about how her party was better than Kelly's but they both had brilliant presents.

'We have lots of sleepovers too.'

'Is there anyone there you don't like?'

'Lottie Pike. She said my feet are big and that means I'm going to be too tall when I grow up and none of the boys will like me.'

'That's a horrible thing to say,' said Goth.

'She always says horrible things to me and Kelly, but mum said to ignore her.'

'Shall we see how she likes it when people are horrible to her?'

Ninja wasn't sure but Goth smiled her encouragement so she thought it would be all right.

Goth concentrated on the items on Lottie Pike's little table in front of her. She hated authority but as much as she wanted, she couldn't do the teacher any serious harm. The eraser should do the trick. While the teacher had her back to the children she quickly picked up the eraser and threw it. It hit the back of the middle-aged woman's head.

'Ouch,' the woman shouted in surprise as she dropped the chalk.

'Who threw that?'

Kelly and another girl had seen the eraser move from Lottie's table but hadn't seen her throw it.

'It was Lottie, miss.'

'No it wasn't,' said Lottie. 'I didn't do it.'

'She did, miss. I saw it too,' Marie added.

'I did not, miss. Honestly.' Lottie was trying her best not to cry.

'Shall we see who has erasers in front of them and who doesn't?' Miss Phillips asked. The back of her head was stinging so she was trying to hide her fury. 'Everybody stay where you are and don't touch anything.'

She insisted on all items being laid out on the tables where they could be within easy reach. So a quick check revealed that Lottie's eraser was missing, but all others were present and correct.

'What have you got to say for yourself, Lottie?'

'It wasn't me, miss, honestly.'

Miss Phillips removed all other items from Lottie and took them to the front of the classroom. 'Open your books and see how many new words you can read,' she said. 'When I return we will see how well you have all done.'

She took her phone out of her pocket and made a call. Within a few minutes another member of staff had arrived.

'Come with me, Lottie,' Miss Phillips said. 'We're going to see the head teacher.'

'Ooh, that was naughty,' said Ninja but she still giggled, putting her hand over her mouth as she did so.

'That'll teach her for being horrible to you and your best friend,' said Goth.

'Paul Winston laughed when Lottie was horrible to me too. He's friends with her.'

Goth nodded to Harry.

'Which one's Paul Winston?'

Ninja pointed to the boy. As the children left the classroom when the lesson finished, Paul appeared to trip over nothing. He landed on the floor and banged his head. Paul felt confused but still jumped up as quickly as he could. He felt giddy and fell over again. The stand-in teacher rushed to his aid and steadied him. When she saw the lump starting to rise on his forehead, she held his arm and they headed in the direction of the school nurse.

Ninja opened her mouth in surprise, then covered it with a hand. Her new friends were very naughty but Paul Winston had been horrible to her too. She thought he deserved it but secretly hoped he wasn't hurting too much.

'Shall we teach you some tricks?' Goth asked.

'Yes please,' said Ninja not knowing she was the new apprentice to one of the Devil's most evil souls.

*****

Gabriella and two junior angels were following Zach. Their mission was twofold. They'd been ordered to take the juniors to the cave for them to take over from Ron and Sandy, then they had to find Claire and Raphael, to bring them back to Cherussola. Ron and Sandy were to help them find Claire and Raphael then would appear in front of the Committee where they would be informed of their future. Gabriella knew this was a major test for her. Whatever Claire and Raphael were up to, if she couldn't follow this simple instruction the Committee would lose any faith in her and she would remain a grade three for a long time, or possibly be demoted even further. She had to be firm, stick to the plan and resist any other temptations. She knew it wouldn't be easy.

They were informed of the bad news on arrival at the cave.

'How many,' asked Gabriella ignoring the *I'm in charge look* Zach gave her.

'Impossible to say,' said Ron. 'But enough to do plenty of damage I should think.'

'Okay, change of plan,' said Gabriella.

Zach had heard enough.

'My show, old girl.'

She remembered she wasn't in charge so she shut up and hoped they were on the same wavelength.

'We will change our plan as Gabriella said. Ron, you and Sandy return to Cherussola as quickly as you can. The Committee want to see you anyway so you'll have no trouble getting in to see them to explain what's happened.'

'Why do they want to see us?' asked Sandy.

Schoolboy error, thought Gabriella. *So instead of focussing on the journey, they'll be wondering why the Committee want to see them. That's bound to slow them down.* She kept a neutral expression on her face, knowing the damage was already done so there was nothing she could do to undo it.

56

'Never mind that now,' said Zach. 'Just concentrate on getting back as soon as you can, deliver the news, then do whatever they ask of you.'

Instead of Ron and Sandy showing the ropes to the junior angels, others were allocated to the task so they could leave as quickly as possible.

'Are you going back too?' asked Ron.

'We have work to do first,' said Zach. 'So be on your way and we'll see you on our return.'

Gabriella assumed the Committee's plans for Ron and Sandy would likely change, now that they'd need all hands to the deck to round up the evil souls and return them to the cave. She made it sound so easy but knew it was going to be difficult and not a forgone conclusion that they'd be successful. But they had to be if they didn't want to witness famine, wars and the suffering of many millions of people. One never knew what surprises the Devil had in store and she assumed this time would be no different. Gabriella sighed. The others looked at her, feeling her distress.

*****

After they said their goodbyes, Ron and Sandy were preoccupied during their journey, wondering why the Committee wanted to see them. Distracted, they didn't pay attention to the souls passing to and fro. Had they been alert, it might have made a difference and prepared them for what was to come. By the time they saw them, it was too late. They tried to avoid Goth, Harry and the young girl who was with them but the evils were having none of it.

Goth couldn't believe her luck when she recognised Ron and Sandy as two of her former captors. She would put Ninja's training on hold and start her payback now.

'Well what have we here?' she said. 'Where do you two think you're going?'

Harry was less subtle. While Ron was formulating an escape plan, he took him by surprise and gave him a swift kick. Ninja couldn't believe what her new friend had just done as Ron went whizzing off into the atmosphere.

57

'That was horrible,' she said.

'Shut up, kid. We have history…'

'He told me to shut up.' Ninja knew that was rude and she'd get a telling off if she spoke to anyone like that.

Goth gave Harry a look, warning that she'd be having words later. 'Grab Sandy, quickly,' she ordered him.

Sandy saw the plan and attempted to get away, but she was too slow and was overcome by Harry's strength.

Goth put a reassuring arm around Ninja. 'I'm sorry you had to see that but these people are bad and need to learn they can't get away with being horrible. They are unkind to people.'

Ninja thought about it for a few seconds. 'Like Lottie and Paul?'

'Exactly, Ninja.'

'She's lying, sweetie,' shouted Sandy as she struggled to break free from Harry. 'They are the evil ones, not me and Ron. We wouldn't hurt…'

'And they lie,' said Goth. 'You can't believe a word they say, Ninja. But you'll be safe with me and Harry, we'll make sure they can't hurt you.'

'Why did Harry kick that man then shout at me?'

'He was concerned for your safety and didn't want the bad man to take you away.'

Ninja wasn't keen on Harry but was glad he'd stopped her from being taken by the bad man. Perhaps he wasn't so bad after all.

Goth nodded towards Harry when Ninja wasn't looking. Sandy was still struggling but he had her under control. 'I know him, Ninja and know he's taken children away before and they haven't returned,' he put on his most sycophantic voice. 'I'm sorry for shouting but was worried about you.'

'It's okay,' she said.

'Harry has to take this woman to our boss now so he can punish her for being bad and stop her from hurting anyone else. He's going to ask our boss what he wants us to do too.' The last was an order for Harry to discover what the Devil wanted them to do next.

'Where is he taking her?'

'Hell, sweetie. He's going to take me to Hell and torture me when I get there. Go and get help, please.'

Knowing what was in store for her Sandy doubled her efforts. Harry was stronger and quickly regained control. He didn't want to use extreme violence in front of the kid but would do so as soon as she was out of sight. He nodded to Goth and made a move, disappearing shortly after.

*****

Claire and Raphael were ready to make their way back. Tired and resigned to the fact they were in a heap of trouble, Claire hoped her intervention had saved Libby so knew it had to be worth it.

'Thank you,' she said as she wrapped Raphael in a hug. It wasn't only for his help with Libby, but for going against his seniors, especially the Committee, knowing there would be consequences for his actions.

He looked at her as they broke apart. 'We are a team, my love, and in this together. And anyway, it was the right course of action. Had it not been, I would have counselled otherwise.'

He loved and supported her and would keep her out of trouble if she was being headstrong, but also help bring her plans and ideas to fruition if he thought she was right. She had truly met her soul mate and looked forward to an eternity with him, whether in the lousy cave or carrying out more pleasant duties.

'Shall we?' asked Raphael. She took the hand he offered as they whooshed off into the darkness to face whatever punishment the Committee deemed appropriate.

They weren't long into the journey when they both noticed the change. There were more souls in the atmosphere and the colours of the orbs indicated they weren't the good guys. There was never peace on Earth, but the relative peace in the time since God and the Devil had had their latest run-in meant that no major wars or

59

calamities had happened since. The balance between good and evil had been with good but now they wondered if that was about to change. Claire was glad she hadn't recognised any of the souls flying past them, and that none of the lights shone enough to show that these were powerful. She wasn't sure she had the strength for a fight.

*****

The kick from Harry had been so forceful that it took a while for Ron to slow down, then stop. He was worried for Sandy, knowing the two evils were stronger and she wouldn't be able to escape without his help. As he was about to move again, two angels appeared in his peripheral vision. He recognised them as they got closer.

'Oh thank the Lord,' said Ron. 'I need your help. We need your help.'

'Hello, Ron,' said Claire. 'What's happened and where's Sandy?'

Ron quickly explained.

'We can get more details later, but first we need to get to Sandy,' said Raphael. He didn't add *before it's too late*, but that's what they were all thinking.

Travelling faster than warp speed, they soon came upon the enemy.

'Goth-Roach,' said Claire. 'And who's this child that you're no doubt trying to poison.'

She hated that name and it took all of Goth's willpower not to scream and attack the angel Claire. She was top of her revenge list. She knew she'd lose the kid if she went all out now and she had plans for her, if the Devil permitted. The child looked confused. Goth knew the effect the presence of angels could have on unbroken souls, so needed to get away if she wanted to keep the child.

'Hello,' said Ninja to the beautiful people with wings.

'Hello,' said Raphael. 'I think you should come with us.'

'They're bad people,' said Goth. 'They'll hurt you if you go with them. We have to leave now.'

60

Ron was in a dilemma. He knew the longer they stayed to sort out Goth-Roach and attempt to steal the child, the less chance they'd have of catching that scumbag Harry and saving Sandy. They might be able to stop this child from going to Hell but his existence would be miserable and pointless without Sandy. Although it made him feel guilty and selfish, he admitted that Sandy was his priority.

The decision was taken out of their hands as Goth-Roach quickly grabbed the child and disappeared with a whoosh. After their work with Libby, Raphael and Claire didn't have the energy to follow Goth-Roach, fight her, and to save the child. Despite this, Claire gave chase but was unable to catch the evil. It was frustrating and distressing watching the young soul disappear with someone so evil. Returning to the others, they vowed to find the youngster when they had the strength, save her and put an end to Goth-Roach once and for all.

Time had passed but they still knew there was a better chance of catching Harry, the weaker of the two, so there was a very slim possibility they could still save Sandy. The three joined hands and sped away, as fast as they could.

It was tantalisingly close. They could see Harry up ahead but were nearing the danger zone; the space where good souls feared to tread. They pulled up as they heard Sandy's screams. Then they saw the hands, which must have caused her distress. Claire tried to shield Ron to stop him from looking but he was like a rabbit in the headlights, watching in morbid fascination as the woman he loved was taken to Hell for the second time.

The bloody and broken gnarled hands grabbed her roughly and pulled her downwards into the dark. Her last image of Ron was his tortured face with tears streaming down it. Claire and Raphael were holding him back as he attempted to follow. This made her smile in the midst of her terror. The fact that Ron loved her enough to follow her to Hell.

Chapter 8

The Devil was delighted to see Harry and hear the news that the cave had been breached. He was even more pleased that Harry had brought him a gift. He ordered a trusted evil to guard Sandy. He had plans and issued orders that no others were to touch her until he had done his work.

Harry tried to take the credit for returning with Sandy but the Devil knew he was a follower not a leader. A little not so gentle persuasion ensured Harry told his evil master about Goth, the child soul Ninja, and Goth's plans before returning to Hell. The Devil approved though would punish Goth for not checking with him first. He wondered if it was coincidence that her plans for the child were very similar to his own plans, only on a much smaller scale. There was no time to think of that now, he wanted to get his show on the road but wanted a bit of fun too. Now that the balance was changing in his favour, there was no reason he couldn't do both. He decided he would amuse himself for a while, after giving Harry his mission.

The Devil sent Harry back up. His orders were to gather the souls who had escaped from the cave and to bring them back as soon as possible. His master didn't need to tell him what the consequences of failure would be. Harry had already seen his father, Big Ed, destroyed for all eternity and certainly didn't want that to happen to him. Any existence was better than none and death was good at the moment. Any freedom from the life of a cockroach in a big dark cave was an improvement.

*****

Sandy was surprised she hadn't yet been tortured. This was her second time in Hell and she knew she wouldn't be pain free for long. She'd been returned to her human form. If the last time was anything to go by, she could expect her flesh to be ripped from her, maybe her eyes gouged out, or perhaps to be eaten by hideous creatures. It was Hell after all and as much as her thoughts were matter of fact, she was absolutely terrified. When she was overcome by mental anguish, she did attempt to escape, but each time she moved outside a three step circumference invisible flames licked at her skin. The evil guarding her simply smiled. A smile that never reached his black, shark-like eyes.

Then he came and her reality was worse than she could ever have imagined.

Sandy heard a noise behind her and instinctively knew her thoughts would soon turn to reality. She turned and couldn't believe her eyes. Ron was standing in front of her smiling. Confused she wondered how he'd got to Hell without being caught by any demons or sent to a torture chamber. Throwing caution to the wind she moved towards him and was surprised again. There was nothing to stop her, her skin wasn't burnt or seared. The angels must have overcome at last, she thought as she ran to him. Sandy threw her arms around Ron and held him tight in a fierce hug, never wanting to let go. She kissed him long and hard and he kissed her back, fuelling her passion. By the time she realised the kisses weren't Ron's, it was too late. The cruel reality hit as she smelled burning flesh and felt her lips sizzle. She watched as they disintegrated slowly, then fell to the floor. The Devil took one of her hands in his. He bent towards it then looked up at Sandy. Ron's brown eyes turned a bright red and she had to look away. He kissed each finger in turn. She screamed as the skin peeled away. Smelling her own hot searing flesh, Sandy vowed to become a vegetarian if ever she returned to Earth in another human life. As he kissed each part of her body, so her skin turned to a burnt crust then dropped off. He bit into one of her breasts then Sandy looked at her now deformed body. One breast had completely disappeared and he licked the nipple on the other, before making his way back up to her neck, then to her face. It was worse than her last time and the pain was unbearable, still he wouldn't put her out of her misery and finish it. She knew she was being punished for not bending to his will the last time she was here, but now wondered how she had managed to refuse him.

He laughed then licked his tongue around his lips. Sandy groaned and pleaded as the Devil kissed one of her eyes. The smell of burning was overpowering but she couldn't escape as she heard a pop and watched in horror as her eye landed on the floor. The other soon followed and she was glad she couldn't see what was happening when his greedy tongue made its way down her body to her remaining breast then further still, to her very core.

The pain was such that Sandy hoped this was the end of her existence. But it wasn't to be.

She didn't know how long she'd been out of it when she came round again, back in her human body. Sandy groaned, knowing that he'd given her body back only to destroy it once more. The torture had been worse than anything she could imagine so she didn't bother to wonder what would happen this time.

She didn't have to wait long to find out.

The gnarled hands that had dragged her to the pits of Hell appeared in front of her. They grabbed, poked and prodded then started nipping her skin. Sandy looked down at her naked form as more and more scabby and broken hands appeared. It felt like she was being pinched a thousand times and she screamed. She knew nobody was coming to save her but hoped it would give release from the pain. It didn't. She should have passed out with the pain but every time she closed her eyes she was slapped awake again. Forced to open her eyes then to look at her body, which she didn't recognise, all she could see was a skeleton covered in a red bloody mass. Any skin that was left was hanging in torn red shreds. Her last thought before losing consciousness was that she was beginning to lose her mind.

*****

Louisa's parents were distraught. Their eleven year old daughter had stabbed and killed a man who had refused to pay her enough for dealing drugs! Their lives had turned into a nightmare and as they sat in the closed courtroom, they weren't surprised when the judge sentenced Louisa to ten years in a children's secure psychiatric facility. They didn't know their daughter any more but had some hope the doctors might be able to treat her.

The professionals initially diagnosed Louisa as schizophrenic. She was two different personalities. The dark one, which Louisa called the killer, was foul mouthed and vile, showing no remorse. When this person was not in her head, Louisa was what the professionals considered a normal child. Pleasant, helpful and industrious, and able to talk to the psychiatrist.

'It wasn't me who killed the man. I know it sounds crazy but another person is in my head making me do things I don't want to do. He is the killer.'

'Why do you call him *he*, Louisa?' Dr Grayson asked.

'You're going to think I'm mad, but he told me his name is Luke, he's twenty-three, and he was in a gang. They all did what they wanted to do and he died of a drug overdose.'

'So Luke told you all of this?'

'Yes, and he's trying to come back now, so help me. Please.'

Dr Grayson pressed the panic button then watched as Louisa's face became contorted as she struggled with her inner demons. It seemed to the doctor that the secondary personality won the struggle when the child spoke.

'You are getting it, you fuckin' bitch.'

The nurse and security staff stormed in and the strong men restrained her, before she had a chance to kick off. They still had bruises from her last outburst so knew to take no chances.

The nurse emptied her syringe into Louisa's arm and she was asleep in a matter of seconds.

*****

Nobody got a second chance with the Devil unless it was to his benefit. His intention was to play with Sandy until she bored him. After tasting and stripping her delicious skin, he watched as the gnarled hands did their work. He licked his fingers recalling the exquisite taste of her but knew it would now be bitter and rancid after everything he'd put her through. Losing interest in his latest victim after he'd had the best of her, he decided to allow his minions to determine her fate. They chose to make her suffer elsewhere for a while.

Sandy's first incarnation was as a wasp. She had been forewarned and told her minimum sting count was two hundred. All the stings had to be delivered to separate people and for each one less than her two hundred, the punishment would be more severe on her return.

She found herself on a playing field amongst a few adults but mostly children. She heard one or two adults bark orders as the children did as they were told, so Sandy assumed it was a school sports event.

She hated being in the body of a wasp. Unsurprisingly she was a junior so had to suffer the cruelty of other wasps as well as the Devil's servants. Sandy also hated inflicting pain on people. Even knowing she would suffer more pain and humiliation when returned to Hell, she expected to find the task difficult. But being a wasp seemed to bring out the worst in all souls so she was able to sting a few adults she'd heard make nasty comments without remorse. The children were a challenge. The other wasps were inflicting their own type of pain on her and it became obvious these were bad souls, who had been ordered to torment her. She wasn't sure whether it was worse being a wasp or enduring the torture in Hell, the pain was pretty even at that time. While two teams were playing rounders, some other children were sitting on the grass, watching the game. Sandy was pushed towards a child who was sitting down, leaning up against a tree, and ordered to sting him. He was away from the other children who were not involved in the game and seemed to be in his own world. He had one arm in a sling and was using the other to play on his tablet. Sandy guessed he was about ten or eleven years old. She landed on his injured arm, climbed up his forearm and stung him. He screeched then jumped up. The noise from the sports field drowned out his shouts and it wasn't until the whistle went that one of the other children noticed the boy had gone an unusual colour. The anaphylactic shock had

66

happened quickly and Sandy watched in horror as the adults ran to him. She knew it was too late when she saw the light leave his body.

'Oh, no,' she shouted but it came out as an angry buzz as she landed on the tree trunk. It was the last noise she made before her body was squatted to a pulpy mess. As her soul left the wasp she was quickly gathered by evils she didn't recognise. It wasn't long before the gnarled hands had hold of her again and delivered her to the pits of Hell for the next round of torment and torture.

The Devil's work was almost done. He could see she was losing any sense of self so this time she would be compliant and soon become one of his servants.

He noted with satisfaction that the balance was changing in his favour. Harry had followed his orders to the letter by delivering many of the escaped souls back to their rightful home. They had been punished appropriately but lightly for delaying their return; he didn't want to damage them before sending them on their important tasks. Careful selection followed and the Devil only gave the possession jobs to those evil souls who were strong and clever enough to do his bidding.

This wasn't going to be full-scale war but chaos would reign, the dark would again dominate and his numbers increase.

He got to work.

*****

Libby and Cassie returned to the centre after their marketing campaign. It had been a successful day with a large donation from a local business and the community magazine whose editor had agreed on a free, two-page spread. They were buzzing as they walked alongside the kennels, looking for staff to discover which dogs needed walking.

'Well who have we here?' asked Libby as she approached a new puppy. She petted the young German Shepherd and it was love at first sight. She was told his name was Spike and they took him for a walk, along with one of the others. As they returned Cassie watched her friend and the dog. Although Libby loved all of the puppies, there was already an undeniable bond between her and Spike. Libby played with him, ignoring everyone else. Cassie picked up her work bag.

'I have to sort this lot out,' she tapped the bag. 'See you in about ten minutes.'

Cassie had tried to change her ways but the temptation was too great. The office was empty so she logged onto the computer and completed the transaction. As soon as she logged out of the secure banking page, she deleted the Internet history. It was a small amount of money like the last times, so she was confident it would only be traced by an eagle-eyed accountant. Fortunately, there wasn't one at the centre.

When she returned to speak to Libby, she was surprised. 'I've applied to adopt him and they've said yes. I'm going to take him home this weekend.' She grabbed Cassie's hands and skipped around, forcing her friend to join in her enthusiasm.

'Are you certain, Libby,' Cassie asked when she'd calmed down. 'You've only just met him.'

'I'm taking a puppy home, not marrying him,' she laughed. 'Besides, we've always wanted a German Shepherd, especially Tony. He's going to love him.'

The initial euphoria now worn off, Cassie asked if she fancied a coffee so she agreed, not wanting to hurry home to Marion's. As much as she loved her mother-in-law, nothing seemed right at home and with Marion's ability to pick up on everyone's emotions, it made her feel uncomfortable. In the months they'd got to know each other, Cassie had been a life-saver and so easy to talk to. She'd listened to her problems without judging and Libby felt much better since Cassie had come into her life. She'd suggested that Libby would be better off moving back home where she could come and go as she pleased without her mother-in-law checking up on her and reporting back to Tony. Cassie had a point and the more she thought about it the more Libby knew it was the right move. She now had the puppy to consider and living in a house with a garden would be better for Spike. Now she just had to pluck up the courage to tell Marion.

'Penny for them?' said Cassie, interrupting her thoughts.

Libby gave Spike one last cuddle and left the caged area. 'Looking forward to taking that little boy home, that's all,' she smiled in the dog's direction and Spike leaned his head to one side, knowing the women were talking about him.

'So cute,' said Cassie and they both laughed. 'But what were you really thinking?'

My God, she knows me so well, thought Libby. 'No flies on you eh?'

Cassie waited.

'I was wondering when to tell Marion I'm moving back home.'

'Well you know my thoughts on that but it's entirely up to you. But you only have a few days if you're planning on telling her before the weekend.'

She had a point, thought Libby, but that didn't make it any easier.

'What about if you took Spike home tonight and just did it?' Cassie was joking, knowing Libby had to buy everything the puppy needed.

'That's actually not a bad idea.'

'I was kidding, Libby. You probably want to tell your husband first.'

'I know that clever clogs,' she touched her friend's arm and both felt the electricity run through them. Without thinking Cassie pulled Libby into an embrace and kissed her on the lips. It took a while before Libby pulled away.

'I... Cassie, I'm married and I love Tony.'

'I know, I'm sorry.' Cassie's hands dropped to her sides. 'I felt something really strong. You can't deny you didn't feel it too?'

69

'Yes, no...' Libby took a deep breath, trying to get her feelings under control. 'It's not right. I'm not that way inclined.'

Cassie laughed at the phrase and put her hands in the air, palms facing Libby. 'Okay, I'm sorry, I misread the signals. Don't worry, it won't happen again. Come on, let's get these cups washed up and get out of here.'

The tension disappeared and they were back to their normal selves. But Libby still had that feeling of excitement in her stomach and knew their relationship would never be the same again.

That made her decision easier. As soon as she had the opportunity to speak to Marion that evening, she would tell her she'd decided to move out. She was a grown woman and didn't need mothering from someone who wasn't her mother.

Marion was eating an early dinner when she heard Libby's key in the door.

'I didn't expect you so early. Have you eaten?' she asked

'I'm not hungry thanks, I had a big lunch.'

She could feel her daughter-in-law's tension but decided not to prompt her. 'How was your day?' she asked.

'Same old, you know. I'll leave you to finish your dinner in peace,' she said before disappearing to her room.

Marion's intuition had been spot on as twenty minutes later Libby returned with two suitcases.

'Are you going home?'

'Marion, thanks for everything. You've been brilliant, but I need to move on and try to...'

'Are you sure this is what you really want, Libby?'

'Absolutely.'

'You know there's a room here for you any time you need it.'

So you can report my comings and goings back to your son, just as Cassie said thought Libby as they hugged.

Marion thought Libby was still fragile and needed her support, but knew there was no point in trying to stop

70

her. As she held her daughter-in-law she felt her tense and sensed this woman was a different person to the one she had known before Val's death.

'Will I see you and Tony this weekend?' she asked.

'I don't think so. Take care and thanks again.'

It sounded almost like a final goodbye and after Libby left, Marion had to keep herself busy to ward off her sense of foreboding.

She should have known by now to trust her instincts.

*****

Polly looked at her youngest daughter who was lying prone on the floor in front of the television. Cartoons were on but Daisy wasn't taking much notice as she was drawing a picture in her colouring book. Ben had taken Millie to her Saturday morning dance class so all was quiet at home. Before the accident, Daisy would have been playing outside with her friends, or asking to go in the pool. She could understand her staying out of the pool after her fright but she'd been in since and hadn't seemed at all bothered.

Yet again she thought about the time since the awful accident. She'd researched similar cases so knew that people could change after a near-death experience, but almost every aspect of Daisy's personality had changed and Polly felt she didn't know the little girl lying in her living room. As ridiculous as it seemed, she was convinced that Daisy wasn't her daughter.

Daisy must have sensed her presence. She stopped drawing and stood up. Walking over to her mother she gave her a hug.

'I've tidied my bedroom, mummy.'

'Good girl, Daisy, thank you.'

'Shall we make cakes for daddy and Millie?'

'What a good idea. We'll need to go to the shops to get the ingredients and you can decide what you want to put on the top.'

'Yippee,' said Daisy and smiled.

As she gathered their things together, Polly reminded herself to record this into the notebook she'd started to keep. There was no way the other Daisy, as she'd started to call her, would tidy her bedroom or want to make cakes. Much as she liked this quiet, kind and gentle version of her daughter, she wished the real one was back with her family.

She later learnt to be careful what she wished for.

*****

Gabriella and Zach had not been able to find Claire or Raphael, and had returned to Cherussola. They were surprised to discover that Ron and Sandy had not yet arrived. Gabriella feared the worst, so Zach went to ask for an audience with the Committee to inform them about the escapees from the cave.

Claire, Raphael and Ron arrived in Cherussola shortly after and were met by Gabriella and Amanda.

'I have to discover what's happened,' said Gabriella.

'And I have to deliver you two to the Committee,' said Amanda nodding at Claire and Raphael, 'and you don't get to rest first.'

Ron was flagging so was sent to rest. He hardly knew where he was and was completely distraught and exhausted after what had happened. Amanda arranged for him to be escorted to his room where he would be out of it for a while.

'Where's Sandy?' Gabriella demanded. In response Raphael asked the same of Zack.

'He's gone to tell them about what happened at the cave. No doubt they're also discussing what to do with you two.'

'I'm hoping they might decide on leniency when they discover what's happened,' said Claire. She went on to explain about the encounter with the evils and Sandy being delivered to Hell.

'It must have been devastating,' said Gabriella, knowing that her brother and Claire would have saved Sandy if they could. They must have arrived when it was too late.

'We have to go,' said Amanda. 'You can tell us the full story later but I hope you had a good reason for not appearing in front of the Committee earlier.'

She left with Gabriella and Raphael held back to have a quick word with Claire. He told her what they should say.

Claire wasn't happy about lying but knew if they told the truth the consequences didn't bear thinking about.

The angel Martin was chairing the meeting and when they were ready to progress he nodded to Zach.

'Where have you been and for what purpose?' asked Zach.

The plan was for Raphael to answer but Claire didn't want him to incriminate himself so jumped in to answer before he could.

'Earth,' she said. 'There was a change in the atmosphere so I wondered if anything had happened at the cave since we'd left. I thought they might need our help. You will see we were proved right when…'

'So you felt the change from here?' Martin interrupted before Claire had finished. When she went to reply he put up a hand to silence her.

'Did anyone else feel a change in the atmosphere?' there was humour in his voice as he addressed the Committee and other attending angels, the implication being that if they did not have the ability to do so, there was no way Claire, with less experience could have. There were negative mutters amongst them all.

'And you Raphael,' asked Martin. 'Did you feel it?'

A subtle look passed between Raphael and Claire. Raphael shook his head.

'What was the real reason for your visit?'

They knew they were busted so Claire decided to come clean, despite their earlier discussion. 'I wanted to save the soul of a poor woman who's suffered enough.' She explained what she had done, leaving Raphael out of the equation.

'And that poor soul is your sister-in-law and Ron's daughter?' asked Zach. 'Is that correct?'

Raphael was fuming that Zach was trying to belittle their cause and using Claire's reasoning as an excuse to improve his own standing.

'That is correct, Zach. I accompanied Claire to assist and ensure she came to no harm. But…'

'I think we've heard enough, old chap,' said Zach. He leaned back in his chair and looked around at the Committee members, like the cat who had the cream, thought Raphael.

'I don't think so,' said Raphael. 'On the return journey we encountered a lost soul who calls herself Ninja. She hasn't been placed due to an error in judgement and the poor thing has been picked up by one of the escaped evils. I wonder who that could be down to?'

Zach paled and it was obvious to all present he was involved.

'What do you know about this, Zach?' asked Martin.

'I have some information for you,' said Zach.' But would like to discuss it with you first before it goes in front of the Committee.'

'I bet you would,' said Raphael.' Claire and I need to be involved in that discussion and so does Gabriella. We all have information you need to know.'

Martin told him to be quiet while he considered Zach's request. He also thought about whether to go through with the punishment the Committee had already discussed for Claire and Raphael. There was no doubt they were in the wrong but it appeared that Zach was too and he couldn't let that go unpunished. With the increase in bad souls, strong leadership was required and at their current grades, they didn't have enough senior angels to do the job. Drastic action was needed but he would have to chat to the Committee first and obtain God's approval. He decided to request an audience and reconvene as required. That part of his decision was the priority so it wouldn't hurt Zach and the others to worry about what their future held.

'We will adjourn for now,' said Martin. 'While The Lord of all Things Good and his Committee consider the way forward. You will be called when a decision has been made. In the meantime,' he made eye contact in turn with Claire, Raphael, Zach, Amanda and Gabriella. 'Nobody is to leave Cherussola. If you do decide to go against my orders, don't bother coming back.'

An intake of breath reverberated throughout the chamber. The consequences of leaving and not being able to return were unthinkable. An angel would be stuck in the ether and soon be picked up by those from the dark side. None of the present company would consider going against Martin's direction for this reason alone.

He was granted an audience and God agreed that Gabriella and Amanda could be reinstated as Grade five and Grade six angels. Although they didn't have all the facts about Zach's so called error of judgement, there was enough for God to know the angel had been promoted beyond his abilities. He was disappointed. Zach had so much potential before the evils kidnapped him and took him to Hell. He was lucky to be rescued and was in the minority in that respect, but they'd expected too much from him. Even so, Zach had to bear some of the responsibility and take his punishment, but God didn't want him to be totally humiliated. He told Martin to send him somewhere where he couldn't do much damage but was out of the way of the current emergency.

'He's suffered more than most would in an eternity. Give him the option to go upstairs if he doesn't want to fight the evils any more.'

Martin had the ideal job for him if he declined the offer of eternity.

'Raphael and Claire, my Lord. What now?'

'They are mavericks just like Amanda and Gabriella, but they're also extremely talented. Let's keep the status quo and recognise their good work, but keep them on a tight rein. Make their orders mission specific and put Gabriella in charge of them. I want Amanda back on the Committee, she's too clever not to be, and I'm ready to forgive,' he drummed his fingers and appeared deep in thought to Martin. 'I want that child to be saved, it will be too hard for Zach to bear if she isn't. I also want Sandy's soul to be rescued. She has suffered too much and doesn't deserve Hell. When she's back, I want her to be given the chance to move on, along with Ron. And finally, I feel the balance changing. We all need to do our best to put it back in our favour. Do you understand?'

Martin understood full well and was so glad that angels were able to perform miracles. It would take many and a big slice of luck to carry out the Lord's orders to his satisfaction.

Chapter 9

'Why don't you like the people with wings? Are they real angels?' Ninja asked questions relating to the angels again and again and it was trying Goth's patience, to the extreme.

'It's not that I don't like them, sweetie, it's just that they pretend to be angels and they're bad people. Really they are.'

'But how can they be if they made me feel warm?'

Goth knew exactly what would make Ninja feel warm, but she had some work for her to do first. She'd already learnt to move small objects so now it was time to move onto bigger and better, but she had to get her into the right frame of mind first.

'I wonder how your family is getting on?'

'I dunno,' Ninja replied, looking as if she would cry any second. 'It's not fair that somebody else is pretending to be me and I'm up here, not allowed to talk to the people with wings.'

It took everything for Goth not to punish Ninja for the slight. The child soul should be honoured to be in her company so Goth was furious she would prefer to be with the holier than thou crew of angels. She would teach them a lesson once and for all. But first she had work to do.

'Would you like to visit your family?'

'Really?' asked Ninja, brightening.

'Come on, hold tight.'

Ninja did as told. Sometimes when they went really fast it made her feel sick so she closed her eyes. The next time she opened them she looked down. Her mother was in the kitchen with the girl who had stolen her body. Daisy was helping her to make cakes and had flour up one arm. Her mum's music was playing in the background and she was trying to coax Daisy to sing along with her. She did eventually but seemed really shy. Her mum laughed, washed her hands then rubbed Daisy's head after she dried them. Daisy looked up at her, smiled, then threw her arms around her in a big hug.

'I love you, mummy.'

Her mother hesitated but Daisy didn't notice. 'I love you too, Daisy.'

They stayed in that position, Polly trying her best to feel the love she used to, and Daisy enjoying the warmth of her mother.

Ninja was furious. She wasn't Ninja and she shouldn't love her mummy. Without any prompting she willed herself into the kitchen. Ninja felt like bashing Daisy with the rolling pin. Using all of her strength she tried her best to move it. Nothing happened. She looked at the bag of flour which was half full, then at the girl who was in her body. She willed it to move and it did. The bag flew the few feet towards Daisy and Polly, the contents spilling over them both.

'What on Earth?' called Polly as she dusted the contents off her arms and Daisy's hair. There must have been a gust of wind but she hadn't felt it. The alternative was unthinkable so that's what she concentrated on telling herself, even though nothing else in the kitchen had moved.

'Mummy I'm scared,' Polly hugged Daisy to her again.

'It's all right, Daisy. We'll go and get cleaned up then go to the shops. Fancy a treat?'

Daisy hated shopping but the thought of a treat tempted her. She smiled at her mother, wanting to please her.

'And now they're going shopping. I want to go shopping,' said Ninja, stamping her spirit feet. She was exhausted from the effort of moving the flour but Goth knew it wouldn't be long before she would be causing bigger and better trouble.

'You will, Ninja. All in good time,' she held her hand to take her back to the ether. By the time they arrived Ninja was already asleep.

Goth had plans to up the intensity of her training. She wanted to return to Hell in the Devil's good books and couldn't think of a better way to do so. Get the new girl to help cause plenty of chaos then deliver the fresh young thing to her master.

He'd be delighted with his new plaything.

*****

Martin held separate meetings. He wanted to give Zach the opportunity to tell his side of the story and knew it would be easier for him in private.

'So what happened?'

Zach explained that Val was ready to enter the baby's body but sadly the infant had died during labour. Ashamed but glad to be able to confess, he told Martin how he'd refused to delay Gabriella's meeting with the Committee so turned down her offer of help, then panicked when it all went wrong.

'I know pride comes before a fall, and this is a perfect example.'

Martin thought for a moment. Zach's habit of speaking with a posh English accent was slowly disappearing and he appeared to be returning to the angel he had been before being taken to Hell and tortured to within an inch of his soul. That was a plus, but the minus was that he had been over-promoted, as God had so rightly pointed out.

'We take some of the blame for your actions?'

Zach's face showed surprise so Martin continued.

'You were promoted too soon following your traumatic experience, and given tasks that were, quite frankly, beyond your ability.'

'I'm not sure it was beyond my...'

'That's the judgement of the Lord, Zach. And I happen to agree.'

There was no point in disputing what Martin said so he remained quiet.

'Your responsibilities are to be taken off you and you should be happier at Grade two. In addition, you have a choice.'

He'd expected demotion so that didn't come as a surprise; he also expected a stint in the cave for a while, but didn't expect a choice of jobs. 'Do tell,' said Zach.

'You either stay and do a stint in the cave as the deputy in charge, or go beyond eternity and know everlasting peace.'

Zach was tempted, but he had more to give. There were more good deeds to do which would help to assuage his guilt about the soul of the young girl.

'Can I help to save young Daisy?'

'Sorry, Zach, but no. Others have already been chosen for that task.'

'Then it's the cave.'

'Good choice,' said Martin. 'I'll make the arrangements.'

*****

Martin knew the second meeting would go well, but kept the others on tenterhooks because they deserved to sweat it out. He let each of them speak in turn, telling their version of events and the reason for their actions. He was impressed with Claire's compassion and kindness, but not by her impatience and would have to speak to Raphael in private, to ensure he kept her out of trouble.

He took his time pretending to consider all the information. Amanda was about to have a go when he looked down from his raised chair and smiled.

'Firstly, Amanda. At the conclusion of this meeting you will be reinstated as Grade six. Although you will go on the occasional mission, it's God's desire that you direct operations from here. So to do this, you are to return to the Committee?'

Amanda couldn't believe what she'd heard. She had been in God's bad books since being removed from the Committee so was overjoyed he had decided to forgive her at long last. She would be the same rank as Martin and no longer required to take orders from him, or anyone else but the Lord. She was delighted, more so at God's forgiveness than her re-promotion. She thanked her lucky stars and whooped in a very un-angel like fashion.

The others laughed, hoping their news was as good.

'Gabriella, you are now re-promoted to your previous rank, but be warned that this is your final chance,' he waited for the words to sink in but she showed no emotion. 'Should you do anything reckless or stupid you'll be moved and not demoted.'

'Thank you, Martin.' She was grateful and a smile spread across her lovely face.

'There will be many difficult situations in future. Always trust your heart to tell you the right way, and whatever you do, ignore temptation.'

'Absolutely.' It was one thing for him to sit there on his gilded chair dispensing his wise words, she thought, but when was the last time he was in the thick of the action and had to make impossible decisions without time to think them through.

'I mean it, Gabriella. Welcome to last chance saloon.'

He must have read my thoughts. Gabriella thanked him again and hoped she wouldn't have to accompany Claire and her brother on any missions. It was usually in their company that she rebelled. She made to take her leave but Martin stopped her.

'Stay awhile, I haven't finished.'

Claire and Raphael wondered if he'd ever get around to them. They feigned boredom but were worried about their future. The worst that could happen would be for them to be separated, whether for a short day or eternity didn't matter, a moment apart felt like an eternity to them both.

Finally Martin addressed Claire. 'The good news is you keep your current ranks and status, with the caveat that Raphael as the senior angel will be responsible for your actions.'

Their expressions showed this news was a pleasant surprise to both. Claire looked at Raphael and wondered whether this was a ploy to test their commitment to each other or to make them fall out by putting Raphael in charge. She quickly dismissed this notion. He had voluntarily helped her with the Libby situation so she saw no reason why he wouldn't at least listen to her future suggestions. Love, respect and trust, as long as they had that by the spade load they could survive anything.

'Do you both agree to abide by this decision?'

'Yes, Martin,' Raphael replied graciously.

You bet ya. 'Yes, Martin,' Claire decided now was not the time for a flippant response.

'You will be sorely tested in your next missions in order to prove you have earned this light punishment.'

Claire didn't like the sound of that.

'And that brings me on to my final task of allocating missions.' Martin lifted the staff. He would have to step down from this seat in the future and hand the power back to Amanda. He therefore decided to make the most of his last actions from upon high. He pointed the staff at Gabriella, Raphael and Claire in turn, making small circles as if pondering which one to talk to first. They all knew that protocol dictated he address Gabriella first as the senior of the three. Amanda rolled her eyes at her daughter and stopped herself from telling Martin to get on with it.

Let him have his moment.

'Gabriella, the Lord God has directed we are to save Sandy's soul. You will therefore direct the mission with assistance from Raphael, Claire, and a host of angels of your choice. The Lord knows how arduous this task will be. Please do your utmost not to lose anyone to the other side.'

They all paled, knowing how hard and dangerous this mission would be. Raphael had already seen Hell and Claire had almost been whisked away by the Devil himself; neither wanted a repeat experience. As frightened as they were, there was no way they could turn down the task.

'Following Sandy's rescue attempt, whether it's successful or not, you will rescue the poor young soul taken by Claire's nemesis Goth-Roach.'

As Martin dismissed them and they left the chamber, they decided to discuss their near impossible tasks. Amanda had to leave them to it as she had Committee duties to fulfil.

Embracing the three in turn, she said her goodbyes and floated away.

'Why can't we save the child first?' asked Claire, not having thought it through properly.

Gabriella nodded at Raphael to explain. 'There's a number of reasons, Claire. All meaning it would be harder to save Sandy.'

She looked confused and he thought for someone so bright, she could sometimes be slow on the uptake.

'There's a good chance he's sent Sandy back to Earth in one guise or another, this will give us a small window of opportunity making it easier for us to rescue her if she's between incarnations. Once the Devil has grown tired of her the reincarnations are likely to cease so we need to get to her quickly. If we rescue the child first, Sandy will likely be kept in Hell and we'll have no chance unless we go there directly. As awful as it sounds, the young soul will still have training to complete. Goth-Roach will want to please her master so won't take her to Hell until she's satisfied she's up to scratch. Experience shows that this takes time.' He sighed knowing that none of them were happy about leaving the young soul with the evil.

Raphael had painted a dismal picture, but at least now Claire understood.

'We're going to have to take these missions separately,' said Gabriella. 'Each one will need all of our strength and concentration. Rest now so you're at your best, then meet me when you're ready to go.' She disappeared with a whoosh.

Claire and Raphael left shortly after, deciding to have a little fun before following Gabriella's advice.

Chapter 10

Basil was offered the job the following Monday. He was delighted, despite being told during his induction week that Katie, the other candidate had suffered a bereavement so would have been unable to accept the post. He was informed his training would need to be on the job as there was some sort of emergency that meant new patients were his priority.

The week following his induction started with an interview with the Director. He still wondered if he had been second choice, a predicament he'd never been in during his life. He gave his ego a slap and brought his attention back to the Director.

The Director had sussed him out. 'You don't need to concern yourself about your position, Basil, you were the first choice.'

'But...'

'I intend to offer Katie another job when her personal life is more stable. It won't be for a while and you will have settled in by then so will be able to show her the ropes. But in the meantime we have an unusual situation you need to be aware of. It's going to be a baptism of fire I'm afraid. Let's go to the conference room and all will become clear.'

Basil looked around while they made their way through the corridors to the conference room. It was the first time he'd seen the school's headquarters and he wondered how they'd managed to keep the place secret from the public who believed the facility was a secure unit for the criminally insane. He recalled something in the papers a while ago questioning this building and another down South, but that had seemed to fizzle out when more important matters hit the headlines – such as the escape and subsequent capture of the serial killer known as Mad Martin.

The twins, Ryan and Janine were already in the room, together with Violet who had recruited him for the job. The pleasantries over, they moved to the coffee station before sitting around the table.

'I gather you know everyone except Janine, who's a key member of our permanent staff,' said the Director. Basil wondered exactly what Janine did as the introductions were made. 'And I understand you had dinner with Jim and Tony on Saturday night?' He had a twinkle in his eyes and the others chuckled.

'Yes. It came as quite a surprise I have to say.'

'How's your cough, Jim,' asked Violet, making Basil realise they were all aware of what had happened.

'That's the only thing that doesn't sit comfortably with this job. Marion has been through a lot during the last few years and I want her to know she can trust me. It doesn't help when I have to lie about my job.'

'Admirable,' said Tony. 'But I'm not sure we agree.'

Even though his mind was on another matter. Basil was amazed that Tony said *we* not *I* as if it was the most natural way to speak. Many twins were close but there seemed to be an extra strong bond between these two that he found fascinating.

'You're right, Basil,' said Jim. 'She has been through a lot, and that's precisely why we don't want her to know anything about what we do here. She'll worry about us. It's only a white lie. It's not like we're doing anything to...'

'I disagree. This is a biggie in my book and...'

'But you knew what you were signing up to,' it was Tony's turn to speak again. 'If we weren't working for the school you would have kept quiet, so what's the difference?'

They have a point, thought Basil. *He has a point*, he corrected himself.

'One of us telling what you call a white lie is one thing, but three of us is completely different and imagine how upset your mother would be if she found out...'

'Four of us actually,' said Fiona as she walked into the room.'

'Oh My God,' said Basil. 'You as well? Is that it or do Marion and Libby work here too?'

'Not yet,' said the Director and the others laughed. Violet was the only one who knew he was deadly serious.

'Now isn't the time to discuss these issues, though I do appreciate your concerns. There are only three families with multiple employees in this school, and they are all currently in this room.'

'We're not exactly family,' said Jim, looking as Basil.

He could be very irritating, thought Basil. 'Not yet,' he replied to wind him up. It appeared to work as the twins didn't know how to respond and looked at each other. Fiona looked down, trying to hide her amusement.

'Well I hope your intentions are honourable,' said Tony. 'We don't want our mother to be...'

'I'm sure Basil's intentions are very honourable,' the Director cut in. 'Now if you don't mind we have work to discuss. You can sort all of this out later.' He hoped at least one of the twins would pay attention during the briefing.

'Most of you know what's going on but for the sake of Basil, I'll just give a quick update. I had lunch with the Police Commissioner last week at his request. He told me that within the last two months, crimes committed by minors have increased by sixty three per cent and are still on the increase. If this wasn't shocking enough, a number of these children seem to undergo personality changes and often don't remember committing their crimes. The worst case was where a thirteen year old was so distraught when reminded she'd set her own house on fire and killed her parents and two siblings, that she later took her own life.'

Basil listened intently. To his knowledge there weren't any new drugs on the street that could affect children in this way, but that wasn't to say there were substances he didn't know about. He asked the question.

'We've carried out our own research,' said Janine. 'It was one of the first things we checked and blood tests show no illegal or unusual substances in their bloodstreams. That goes for all but five per cent of the kids that were checked.'

'Watch this,' said the Director. He pressed a few buttons on the remote and the screen lit up to show CCTV footage of cars on a motorway, going at speed. One car moved suddenly from the middle lane into the slow lane, directly into the path of a heavy goods vehicle. The truck driver braked but couldn't do anything about it as his vehicle crumpled the car as if it was a toy.

'The father was driving and his twelve year old son was in the passenger seat. His wife and six year old son were in the back,' said the Director. 'There were no survivors.'

'Anybody know why?' asked Basil. 'Did he have any history of erratic behaviour, or depression?'

'I'm afraid you're barking up the wrong tree, Basil. Watch this footage.'

One of the other CCTVs had captured some footage from another angle, before the accident. When they zoomed in it clearly showed the boy in the passenger seat picking up a hammer, hitting his father with it and taking control of the steering wheel. The mother and child in the back of the car looked like they were screaming. The mother removed her seat belt and leaned forward, attempting to grab the steering wheel, but it was too late.

The Director nodded to Ryan.

'The police made enquiries about the boy but nobody reported any history of strange or bad behaviour. We also made our own enquiries. His best friend Steven said there was nothing wrong with him until the day of the accident when he'd called him. Steven said he told him he couldn't play football as he had something very important to do, he added that it didn't sound like Brooklyn and he later told his mother that he thought someone else was in Brooklyn's house, and was playing a prank on him.'

'Steven's mother told him not to be silly, until she heard about the accident.' The Director was speaking again. 'She didn't report it to the police because she didn't see the point. The family were dead and it wouldn't bring them back. We've had reports of similar accidents but nothing to prove the child in the front took control of the car. Some of these children are in custody so we'd like your evaluation, Basil.'

'Of course.' Talk about a baptism of fire thought Basil. But he had wanted a new challenge.

It took Sandy a while to remember who she was. The smell hit her and she didn't want to open her eyes. It was rank and the overpowering stench was the filth of fear, but there were others; blood and dirt added to the mix. This was another version of hell on earth. She opened her eyes and looked around. It was like a scene from an animal horror movie and she knew this was no regulated, clinical slaughterhouse. Pigs were in different stages of life and death and the blood mixed with faeces and filth on the floor. So she was a pig, amongst other pigs. Some of them were attempting to run around to escape their human captors. As they did so they bumped into the poor creatures already in their final death throes. She watched as one animal was approached by a man wearing rubber boots and scruffy clothes. He carried a hook and spoke in a language unfamiliar to Sandy. He laughed as he stuck the hook in the animal's mouth and lifted it so the pig couldn't move without experiencing even worse pain. Another man with a large sharp-looking knife approached the pig from behind. He made a cut in its neck from one end to the other. The pig screamed and thrashed around before falling to the floor, shaking and screaming. It seemed an age before the animal quieted but it was still alive, Sandy could see the agony and desperation in its eyes. Initially resigned to the fact this was her inevitable destiny, when the man spoke and approached her, her survival instinct kicked in. It was no good and as she lay bleeding to death, another part of her soul withered away. She struggled to remember who Sandy was and why she was here. Lifting out of the body, the hands took her straight away. She vaguely remembered another time where gentle, soft hands belonging to angels and generous souls spirited her away to a world full of sunshine and kindness. Perhaps that was imagined, thought Sandy knowing her only future was one of relentless pain and torture.

*****

Since Goth had increased Ninja's training, the child was constantly tired and had stopped asking questions about the angels. Like most kids she was like a sponge and as long as Goth kept it fun and interesting, Ninja was engaged and her talents developed. Always impatient, it wasn't quick enough for teacher. Whether or not Ninja was ready for the experience, she decided it was time for the next test...

Polly and Ben were stuck for what to do. Since the flour had moved in the kitchen, there had been other incidents in the home that couldn't be put down to anything logical. The worst was when Daisy's bikini was found in the pool one morning. Daisy either sleepwalked or they had a poltergeist. They concluded that the stress since Daisy's accident must have taken its toll on the whole family so decided to go on a break to the UK to visit family and friends. Polly's father who had already returned home, was delighted at the news. Two weeks later, tired and ready to feel the sun on their skin again, they returned to their villa in Spain.

The girls were collecting their toys, little cases and iPads from the car while their father dealt with the heavy luggage. Polly opened the door and went inside. Her hand flew to her mouth as she entered the living area. The place looked like a hurricane had torn through it and she ran outside.

'Ben, Ben, we've been burgled.'

He ran inside followed by Millie who held her younger sister's hand protectively.

'Call the police and don't touch anything,' said Ben. 'Then take the girls back to the car.'

Polly shook her head knowing what her husband was thinking.

'Go on. Everything will be okay,' he said quietly. Ben rushed to the garage, removed a hammer from his toolbox then quickly went back into the villa.

Seeing her parents' distress, Daisy started crying. Her sister held her tighter and whispered words of comfort, though she was scared too. What if somebody was still in the house?

'Come on girls,' said Polly. 'Nobody's been hurt, they're just things.'

Daisy stopped crying as the girls followed their mother. Their father came out shortly after, just as the police were arriving. They explained they'd been away and the police asked what had been stolen. Their elderly neighbours agreed to look after the girls as Polly and Ben accompanied the police throughout the villa.

'We'll need a list of anything that's missing,' said the female officer in heavily accented English.

As they went through the villa, Polly picking up bits and pieces in each room, it soon became clear that nothing of value was missing.

'So this appears to be an act of vandalism, rather than a burglary. I need the names of anyone who might have a grudge against you,' said the same officer as she took out her notebook.

'I can't think of anyone,' said Polly.

'Nor me. But we do have CCTV so that should help.' Ben had thought Polly was being over-cautious when she wanted the system installed, but had agreed to keep her happy. He was glad he had now. The police asked for footage during the entire time since the family had left for the UK, until their return. While Ben connected up the computer to download the information to a USB stick, the officers went next door to speak to the neighbours, to discover whether they had heard anything. Polly accompanied them to the elderly neighbours' home to check on the girls and to ask whether they could keep them for a few hours while she tidied up with Ben. She didn't want to cause them any further upset but knew if they saw the state of their rooms they would probably have nightmares, especially Daisy.

MY MUMMY AND DADDY was written on one of the walls in Daisy's bedroom, in a big, uneven childlike scrawl.

'What the hell?!' said Ben when Polly called him up to the room. 'Who would break into our home to do this? It doesn't make sense.'

Polly did her best to push her thoughts to the dark recesses of her mind. Voicing them would make them a possibility and Ben would think she'd totally lost it.

'Somebody who wants to mess with our heads, Ben. Who could that be?' Usually strong, this was breaking her and she covered her face with her hands and cried. He held her and made soothing noises until the tears stopped.

'Have we got paint in the garage?' Back to her normal self now, she wasn't going to let anyone or anything ruin her family.

Ben said they had.

'We'd better make these walls our priority. I'll clean the writing off then you can paint over anything that won't come off. We can clean up the rest of the mess while the paint's drying.'

'Yes, sir,' he said. Ben did a mock salute glad his wife was back to her usual self.

They were shattered after they'd finished and took the girls out for a pizza as a treat, hoping to lessen the effect of what they'd seen that morning. But the mess and the writing weren't the only shocks that day. Later, when the girls were sleeping, they discussed what their neighbours had told the police.

'So they thought we were back last night?' said Ben. 'Because Mrs Perry told the police she heard Daisy laugh like she used to before the accident.'

'That's right,' said Polly. 'And he said they were surprised the car wasn't here this morning, so knocked before we got home but there wasn't any answer.'

'It'll be interesting to see what's on the CCTV then. I wish we'd looked at it first before handing it over.'

'Me too,' said Polly. 'I need a drink.'

Two days later it was raining so the girls were playing in their bedrooms when the police returned the USB stick.

'The light was flashing on and off as if someone was in or approaching the property,' said the officer. 'But there's no record of anyone entering of leaving.'

'How can that be?' asked Ben. 'You saw the state of the place with your own eyes.'

'Please, Mr Lester, I'm simply stating the facts.'

'We understand,' said Polly, trying her best to stay calm. 'But there has to be footage. Somebody, or something has been in our home and made this mess, can you check again please?'

'Mr and Mrs Lester, are you absolutely sure your villa wasn't like this before you left and...'

'Don't be ridiculous,' said Polly. Ben wasn't so patient.

'Right that's it. You honestly think we would do this and then call the police for assistance. Get out, go on.'

'Now, Mr...'

'No. There's nothing more to be said.'

He shoed them out of the villa, being careful not to touch either one.

'I don't effing believe it!' Ben said as he slammed the door behind them. 'Do they think we're nutters or something?'

Polly couldn't hide her thoughts any longer. 'Ben, I need to talk to you but you're not going to like what I have to say.'

Later when she'd finished he looked at his wife. Some of what she'd said echoed his own thoughts. 'Look, I know Daisy hasn't been herself since the accident, but it's understandable considering the fact she nearly died. The specialist said this has happened before. Remember the English man who came out of a coma and spoke Portuguese, when he could barely speak his own language? And the woman from Scotland who was convinced she was from Birmingham?'

'I know but...'

'Imagine what her family thought when she sounded like a Brummie?' he laughed.

'Ben, please. This is serious.'

'I know it is, Polly, but what do you want me to say? That our real daughter's dead and is haunting the house while we are bringing up some sort of imposter?'

Polly opened her mouth in surprise. She hadn't said any of that though she'd thought it often, so if she hadn't put those ideas into Ben's head...

'So you think exactly the same as I do. If anyone had said this happened to them before Ninja's accident I would have given them a wide berth. But now?'

'Now we have to deal with the situation, Polly. And I don't know what to do.'

'Me neither, but we have to do something. Perhaps hypnosis?' She got up and headed for the door. 'Can you do the coffees while I check on the girls? Then we'll think about what options we have and what's going to be best for Daisy and the rest of us. I know this has already affected Millie so we need to protect her too.'

When she heard her mother heading for the door, Millie disappeared up to her room as soon as she could. If what they were saying was true, her sister wasn't the same person she was before her accident. Millie wasn't surprised. She'd been thinking the same thing since Ninja, no Daisy she corrected herself, came home from the hospital.

*****

Following a further round of torture in the den of the Devil, Sandy found herself in another incarnation on Earth. She was a hedgehog and had a pain along her back. In her lucid moments her initial thoughts were, *this isn't too bad*, but then she heard the buzzing. She looked up to see a swarm of flies hovering over her, and felt movement on her back. She felt rough and tired, knowing exactly what her fate would be, but wondering how she would get there. The Devil and his servants had creative imaginations and the many different ways to inflict pain and humiliation seemed never ending.

She walked for a while and found herself at the back of some houses where she heard voices. Sandy had no idea where she was heading but kept on walking.

'Oh look, mum, it's a hedgehog.'

On hearing the child's voice, Sandy looked up and saw four humans; two adults with two young boys.

'Poor little thing,' said the woman looking to her husband. 'Is there anything we can do?'

'What's wrong with it, dad?'

'It looks like it's got a cut that's infected, Sam, and the flies have laid their eggs in there.'

'Can we save it?'

'We can try, Callum.'

They cancelled their walk and returned to the house to get what was needed. The father had a box, an old blanket, a few old towels and some fly spray. He sprayed the flies, covering Sandy's eyes as he did so. Then picking her up, he laid her gently onto the soft blanket in the box. It had been a long time since she'd been shown any kindness and she was very moved.

'Aw look, dad, she's crying.'

The man chuckled. 'Hedgehog's can't cry, son,' he ruffled Callum's hair. 'It's probably got an eye infection too.'

'What are we going to do with it?'

'Feed it and make it as comfortable as we can. Then we'll let it get a good night's sleep. Your mother's on the phone now to Uncle John so we'll see what he has to say.'

John was a vet so they would act on his advice.

'What shall we call it?'

As Sam asked the question, a loud clap of thunder resounded. It came from nowhere and made the three jump. The skies turned from a spring blue to dark threatening grey then almost black when the sun disappeared. They had no idea the dark spirits were warning them not to interfere.

'Come on boys, before we get soaked.' The weather forecasters had got it wrong and Chris knew they didn't have long before the downpour. They reached their back door just as the giant raindrops started to fall.

Sandy, or Tiggy as the boys had named her, was as comfortable as she could be with maggots eating her flesh. Uncle John had popped in and crushed some antibiotics into her food. He had also recommend they feed her with a non-fish based cat food and ensure she had plenty of water to drink.

'It'll be touch and go, but she should pull through. I suggest you take her to the Hedgehog Sanctuary as soon as she's well enough. For now keep her warm and well fed, and keep the flies off her. I've removed all the maggots. She's lucky you found her when you did, Rose,' he said to his sister. 'Without antibiotics the poor thing wouldn't have a chance.'

When the family went to bed that night, the flies returned. It was unusual for flies to come out during the hours of darkness, but these weren't any ordinary insects. They laid their eggs, which hatched into larvae almost immediately. Sandy knew that despite the best efforts of the lovely family, she was going to die another horrendous death. The family's kindness had restored her faith that there were still kind people about, who were willing and able to make a difference. Their actions had given her back some strength and a smidgeon of hope. She vowed not to let the Devil's demons destroy what was left of her soul, and hoped with all her being that the good guys would think her worthy of saving.

They made her suffer until the family woke and came downstairs the following morning. Sam was the first into the kitchen and he screamed for his mother.

As her soul left the hedgehog's body, Sandy looked at the mess in the kitchen. All that was left of her host's body was a head, some prickles and bones. The grotesque maggots were fat and lumpy, almost bursting out of their skin. Flies were on every kitchen surface, eating whatever they could.

Rose also took in the scene, and the smell. It was like ten years of sewage mixed in with rotting corpses. She put one hand over her mouth trying not to throw up. Sam had already been sick on the floor and was still heaving. She grabbed him with her other hand, and left the kitchen, closing the door behind them. Rose ran to the bathroom and puked. Telling the children to go to their rooms, she followed them up the stairs and got two tea towels. Chris wrapped one around his mouth and nose and Rose followed suit. They made their way to the kitchen. As gross as it was, Chris took a few photos as he knew his friends and family would think he exaggerated when explaining the scene in the kitchen on that Monday morning.

Things started going wrong for his family a few days later.

*****

Polly and Ben were in the specialist's surgery. They told him about the changes in Daisy but had decided not to mention the graffiti on her bedroom wall, and the other strange events which they would struggle to explain. The doctor sat back in his seat, eyeing them both.

'You will recall I explained what can happen when a person's had a near death experience?' He didn't wait for an answer. 'We have cases with extreme personality changes and even where the patient is convinced they are from another part of the world. It can be confusing and distressing for the family, especially if the patient is a child.'

'We do understand that,' said Ben. 'But honestly, it's as if Daisy is somebody else's child and not ours. Are there any further tests you can do?'

'Polly, Ben, we've already carried out all the tests we can and there is no evidence of brain damage, or any physical trauma for that matter. Daisy has recovered well. Her accident must have been extremely frightening. I would recommend you carry on giving her the love and support you are currently doing. It could be very upsetting to discover her parents think she's not their *proper* daughter,' he opened his hands in a sympathetic gesture. 'I know it's hard but my advice would be to leave it for now. If you find you really can't cope, come back in a month and we'll look at counselling.'

Dissatisfied with the advice, they thanked him and made their way home, wondering if it was they who were losing the plot, and not Daisy.

*****

Goth decided it was time for Ninja to pay Daisy a visit, on an entirely different level. The first time it was important that they got Daisy on her own. Night time, just before going to sleep would be perfect as it would be easier for Ninja. It would become less of an effort for her over time but for now, she would need to practise.

'Where are we going?' asked Ninja.

'To see your family,' Goth smiled.

'But it makes me cry to see that girl pretending to be me. I don't want to.'

'It's going to be different this time. I'll show you as soon as we get there,' she added, pre-empting Ninja's question.

Daisy had had her bath and it was Polly's turn to read her a story. This was new as Ninja had liked to play on her iPad before going to sleep, rather than hear fairy tales. Ninja frowned as she saw her mother stroke the other girl's head then give her a kiss before leaving the room. Daisy was at that delicious place between wakefulness and sleep as her mother switched on a dim light that Ninja noticed was new. Many things were changing and she wasn't happy.

'How would you like to be back down there?' asked Goth. 'Back in the body that belongs to you?'

'Really?'

'Yes, really.'

'Yes please,' her frown disappeared and Ninja smiled.

'I want you to think really hard about being back in your body,' said Goth. 'Imagine moving your arms and legs, looking through your own eyes, blinking, sneezing, breathing...'

'But...'

'No buts, Ninja. When you can really imagine doing all of that, I want you to whizz down there and fly into your body. You have to be very quick, do you understand?'

She nodded.

'Good. Now the other girl will still be there. You will feel very tired first of all so when the other girl speaks to you, ignore her. I need to know that you've been able to do it, so as soon as you're back in your body, give me the thumbs up like this.' Goth demonstrated. 'Are you ready?'

'Nearly.' Ninja closed her eyes and did everything Goth had told her.

Goth watched as Ninja's soul entered her former body.

Daisy felt the change straight away and was instantly awake.

Ninja did her best to ignore her and tried with all her might to lift her hand in a thumbs up gesture.

'Gggeeeettttttt out of meeeeeee!' Daisy sat up in bed and screamed.

Millie jumped off the settee in the living room and approached the stairs. 'I'll go,' said her father. 'Stay here with your mother.'

Millie knew it meant trouble if her father took control. She'd felt protective of her sister since the accident and wasn't happy staying put. Something strange was happening in their home and she wanted to know what was going on. Polly obviously felt the same as she took hold of Millie's hand while her father went up the stairs, then mother and daughter followed without a word.

They all watched for a moment, mesmerised, from outside the bedroom. Daisy lifted her right hand and her left hand brought it back down. There was a fierce, but determined expression on her face as she did so. Then her right hand lifted again and it looked like an immense effort as her fist opened and she unfolded her thumb then lifted it in a *thumb's up* gesture. To her father, mother and sister, it looked as if Daisy was two people, each fighting for dominance. The thumb's up lasted for a nano second when Daisy's left hand pulled the right hand back down. When the right hand slapped Daisy's face, her father intervened. He ran to the bed and held his daughter in a hug, preventing her arms from moving. He felt as if he was fighting his daughter and he didn't know what to do.

'It's all right, Daisy, everything's going to be all right,' said Ben, trying to convince her as well as himself.

'It's Ninja, daddy. I'm back.'

A shiver went up Ben's spine as he tried to understand what was going on. Whatever it was, he had to be strong for his daughter.

Something changed and her body lifted from the bed then collapsed back onto it. She seemed to change colour then the light left her and she started to breathe normally.

Daisy opened her eyes and looked at her father. 'Somebody was in my head, daddy. I'm scared.'

Ben was scared too. He leaned over and gave her a kiss, not trusting himself to say anything.

*****

Goth took Ninja into her arms and flew away into the atmosphere. The child had exceeded all of her expectations and was exhausted beyond measure. This was just the start and Goth was already planning future incursions to cause chaos amongst the family and their friends. She knew it was time to inform her master but didn't want to take the child to Hell until she was fully trained and ready. It was time to find Harry. She needed him to deliver her update to the Devil. She knew her master would be pleased with what she was doing with Ninja, but had to think of a good excuse for not yet delivering her. She flew around to the usual hangouts of other dark souls and soon discovered Harry's whereabouts.

Ninja was still out of it and would be for some time, so Goth held onto her protectively. She explained how far the child had come and the recent possession of Daisy's body.

'The Devil will be impressed,' said Harry.

'I know but I should have taken her to him by now. I want...'

'No you misunderstand,' Harry interrupted. 'My orders came directly from our master. I had to find as many as I could who escaped from the cave, and tell them to return to Hell. The Devil hand picked those he wanted to return so that they could possess children and cause chaos. You've fallen in with his plans without even knowing it.'

Goth was relieved and extremely happy. But she knew he would still expect to see Ninja so needed to deliver a message. 'I want you to take him a message, Harry. Tell him that this child has natural talent and will be exceptional if trained properly. Beg his patience and tell him I don't wish to waste his time. I will bring her to him, when she is fully trained and good enough to meet his needs and desires.'

Harry hadn't planned on returning to Hell for a while, but knew if he refused Goth she would punish him over and over, until she was bored with him. There was no point in arguing. The Devil would no doubt have a message for her so it would be good to hang out with her and the child on his return, and witness what Ninja could really do.

'Will do. I'll join you guys on my return, then I can help when Ninja's in this state.'

Goth didn't respond and sent him on his way.

*****

It was Tuesday morning and Marion had just returned from a run. The twins had encouraged her when she said she was joining a running club and so had Basil. The only one who'd taken the mickey was Melanie, saying she must be going through a mid-life crises. Marion had laughed. Mel, who she loved as if she were a blood relative, was probably right. Marion had been nervous at first but wasn't the only beginner and had already started to feel more energetic after only three weeks.

Following her shower, she sat down with her cup of tea and reflected on Saturday night's dinner. The twins' reaction had been weird when Basil arrived and knowing her boys as she did, Marion wondered what they were hiding. Come to think of it, Basil had seemed initially surprised too, and Fiona also looked like she had a secret. But to be fair, thought Marion, Fiona often looked mysterious, like she was hiding something. As the radio played in the background she tuned out. The only one who hadn't been surprised was

100

Libby so she wasn't in on it. Marion came to the same conclusion that had hit her on Saturday night. She'd been trying to find another one since then, but her thoughts had been going round and round in circles and always returned to the same verdict. The twins and possibly Fiona already knew Basil before he arrived at the house. Obviously they didn't know that Basil and Marion were an item. So where had they met and what were they all up to? Most importantly, why did they need to keep it a secret? She had no idea how to find out without asking directly, but find out she would.

The phone rang bringing Marion back to the present. It was Melanie.

'I can't come shopping on Saturday, Auntie Marion.'

'Oh, that's all right, sweetie, what are you up to?' She could hear the excitement in Mel's voice so tried to hide her disappointment. Marion loved her outings with the teenager who reminded her so much of Claire, her own beloved daughter.

'Dad's in a competition in Spain again, and he's booked surprise tickets for me, for my birthday, while mum is staying with Auntie Sylvie to recover. Mel explained that her mum Carol was undergoing minor surgery the following week, then got back on to the subject of her father and Spain.

'He's got a really good chance of winning this one so I can watch him in the finals and spend time sightseeing and sunbathing if it's hot enough which I'm sure it will be. I know it sometimes rains this time of year but dad said some of the days are more like summer than spring and will be warm enough for me to swim. If the weather's not good I'll do my studying.'

She was waffling so Marion let her continue. Mel was on the half-term break from university. She worked so hard, a holiday would do her the world of good.

'We'll go shopping when I get back, that's if you can fit me in?'

Marion laughed, Mel's excitement was infectious. 'Oh I'm so busy I'll have to check my calendar. Of course I can fit you in. Have a lovely time and give your mother my love. Say hi to your dad too and wish him luck in the competition.'

Now it was Mel's turn to laugh, knowing that the history between her father and adopted auntie meant Marion wished him anything but luck. She still adored the older woman though. 'Will do and I'll phone you.'

'Thanks, sweetie. Have fun.' They hung up and Marion wondered about Basil again and what he was doing that weekend. He said he was working so they wouldn't be seeing each other. In fact, the twins and Fiona were working and God knows what Libby would be up to. Thank goodness for the running club, she thought, now that her family were all otherwise engaged. A fleeting thought made her wonder if the twins and Basil's jobs were connected. Marion intended to find out, sooner rather than later.

Chapter 11

The shock and strain of recent events were taking their toll on Polly, Ben and their girls. Millie was nervous around Daisy and her parents were distracted, as if they were all waiting for something to happen. The day after the bedroom incident, Daisy woke up withdrawn and frightened. However, as the day progressed, she became bright and cheerful in her own reserved way and was more relaxed than her parents and sister. It seemed to Ben as if she was watching out for them, instead of the other way around. They needed some air so decided on a walk along the beach after breakfast.

As the girls were checking out the stones, and trying, without success, to dodge the waves, Ben reached out to hold his wife's hand and looked at her face. She was probably thinking the same as him as her forehead was set in a deep frown and he noticed the fine lines on her face that hadn't been there before Ninja's accident. Daisy, he corrected himself for his lapse. The child who'd been happy to be called Ninja since she could talk, would now only answer to her given name. Polly gave him a weak smile then both parents looked at their girls. Before the accident Ninja would have been the first to run into the sea, fearless and full of life, she was now completely different. Millie led the way and her sister reached out for her hand if a dog ran along the beach or if a wave got too close. Millie appeared to take it all in her stride but her parents knew it was affecting her too. Daisy was also more thoughtful these days. The first to pick up on any changes of mood in the house and the first to volunteer for any chores, unlike her former self who would have a drama queen tantrum if told she must tidy her bedroom or do her homework when she didn't want to do it. She still liked to play on her iPad occasionally, but preferred reading and drawing. She was definitely a changed person and it was as if they were fostering another child. At the same time, both parents thought she was a different child and although they couldn't explain it, knew they were absolutely right.

'We need a distraction.'

'Pardon,' said Polly, still lost in her own thoughts.

'We have to make a decision about what to do next, but before we do, we need a distraction.'

Polly looked at him, knowing more was to come.

'The three months or so since the accident have been so intense, Polly, it's like we're in our own world. Although we've seen the specialist and know we have to do something, I think we, as a family, need a timeout.'

'Timeout?'

'Yup. Some fun time and a break from all this intense stuff. You and I need to make a decision that's going to affect us all but before that, we need some fun like we used to have.'

'Fun,' she attempted a smile. 'I remember that.

They couldn't afford a proper family holiday, but lived and worked in Spain so didn't need to go far.

'Lee's competing in La Manga the week after next, how about we head down there for a few days?' Ben's brother was a successful weight-lifter and they didn't get to see him very often. His daughters loved watching their uncle and all the other competitors and it was something the whole family enjoyed.

'That sounds great, Ben, but I doubt we could afford the accommodation.'

'Well,' said Ben. His wife smiled, recognising that he'd already checked it out.

'Spill.'

'You're right, I've spoken to him and he's booked it already. He says it's his treat and he wouldn't take no for an answer. You know how he loves an audience and if we don't go he could lose his deposit. The whole family are going Polly, it's the first time I'll have got together with both of my brothers, and mum and dad in ages. And anyway, it will give the grandparents a chance to spoil the girls which means...'

'Some time on our own, if your brothers don't hijack you,' she laughed. He didn't need to convince her, Polly was

104

looking forward to it already. 'Shall we tell them or keep it a surprise?'

'You know how they love watching Lee, Polly, and spending time with Dean and mum. Let's tell them now.'

'Girls, we have news. Guess where we're going the week after next?'

They eventually stopped guessing, but their parents' excitement was infectious and they giggled in anticipation.

'La Manga, to see your Uncle Lee and lots of others in a weight-lifting competition. Your Uncle Dean and grandparents will be there too and there's also a strong man and strong woman competition on at the same time,' said Ben.

'Yippeee,' said Millie. 'That's great.'

'Who's Uncle Lee,' asked Daisy.

Ben felt like a deflated balloon. His good mood disappeared like a dark cloud passing over the sun. By the look of Polly and Millie, they felt exactly the same.

*****

In Scotland Basil stretched between appointments and got himself a strong, black coffee. He was in C Wing and had been asked to assess whether this morning's patients had mental illnesses or whether something more sinister was at work. The two teenagers he'd already seen had been surly and uncooperative. It had been his first appointment with each and it wasn't unusual for patients to take a while to open up. He would type up his written notes later but hadn't detected anything unusual in either. He assumed the next appointment would be more difficult. He was to see the girl the twins had apprehended. The *Psycho Stabber* as the press had named her.

He'd been offered protection during the appointment. From his vast experience, Basil knew patients were more likely to open up during one-to-one sessions so had declined. Somebody would be right outside the room watching the interview; if she did decide to have a pop at him, they would be able to help if required. He gave himself a mental shake. She was an eleven year old child for God's sake, unarmed and medicated. What could she possibly do to hurt him? Then he reminded himself that she had stabbed and killed a man.

Louisa sat down opposite Basil as instructed and smiled. It seemed genuine and as he talked to her about her family and friends the girl appeared relaxed and pleasant. As he made his notes he wondered if she were schizophrenic. She certainly didn't present as psychotic and he had to keep reminding himself that this pleasant child was a murderer. Apparently she had never used drugs in her life and he wondered if she was lying. He asked her to take him through the day when she killed the drug dealer.

Without warning she leaped from her chair with a screech and put both her hands around his throat. She hit him with such force that Basil fell to the ground still on his chair, while the girl squeezed tighter and tighter. He knew that adrenaline fuelled anger or madness could give someone extra strength, but this wasn't the strength of an eleven year old girl, more like that of a fully-grown man, and a strong one at that. Basil clawed at her hands but couldn't budge her steel-like grip. Two guards and a nurse came flying through the door. The guards tried to restrain Louisa but she was like a wild animal. It wasn't until the nurse put the needle in her arm that Basil felt the child's grip loosen before her body slumped on top of him. Whilst Basil took a few seconds to control his breathing, the guards took Louisa away as the nurse righted her chair.

'Sit here,' she said to Basil, holding out a hand to pull him up. 'You're going to have a nice bruise there, and there,' she pointed to both sides of his neck. 'How do you feel?'

'More shocked than anything else but I felt the impact in my back when I hit the floor. Lucky for me she was too busy gripping my neck so my head didn't bang the floor too hard. I need to speak to the Director.'

'Not until after you've been to the surgery and the doctor's given you a proper examination.'

Although he didn't know the nurse, Basil recognised the look on her face from many others he had known. There was no point arguing so he did as told and made his way to the doctor's surgery.

*****

Here we go again thought Sandy as her soul waited for the ghoulish hands to drag her to Hell and the pits of despair. For every gnarled and scabby hand that touched her, came another warm, soft and gentle one. Sandy was under no illusion. She knew this was the Devil's way of playing his games. He enjoyed giving souls hope then stripping it away just as they began to consider the possibility of a better, happier existence. Even when she felt herself rising, such was her state of mind that she still didn't consider the angels and other good guys might have hold of her and were taking her somewhere better. The balance changed again as the amount of gnarled hands doubled then trebled and her journey stopped. She felt like a tug of war rope being pulled one way then the other, only this time it was up and down. Sandy opened her eyes to see Gabriella right in front of her.

'Feel free to join in,' said the angel.

Knowing this was a proper rescue attempt Sandy joined the frantic struggle, trying to move as many of the nasty hands as she could. Even when others replaced them she vowed she was making progress and wasn't giving up; her future depended on it. She was too busy to see Claire and Raphael in the distance with a number of other souls fighting off more and more demons. Their circle of love moved towards Sandy and the others and soon enveloped her. One angel had let go and the demon hands saw the break in the circle. They attempted to grab the angel's foot but he lifted both feet out of their reach, the fear giving him strength and impetus to whoosh back and re-join the circle.

Gabriella could see others heading their way and knew disaster was in the offing if they didn't move now.

'Eyes closed, concentrate. Let's go,' she said. They disappeared with a whoosh before the dark souls could catch them. The demons gave chase but started to weaken the further up they went. As angels weakened on the journey down to Hell, so did the dark souls heading in the other direction, whether it was to Cherussola or beyond.

*****

When Harry gave Goth the news she was raging. Just when the momentum was swinging back in their favour, their master had lost one of his latest playthings. His minions who'd been allowed to torment her would be bored and the Devil would have to use more imaginative ways to control them. Goth knew he'd be furious and spoiling for blood. She also knew she wasn't in his good books. It was pointless taking the child there now. He would take his fury out on her and likely destroy her. All Goth's training would be a waste of time.

Initially, her plan was to wait for passing good souls or angels to take her fury out on. She still had the hated Claire in the back of her mind, and delivering that bitch to the Devil would be the icing on the cake. Goth tried to calm herself, knowing she couldn't think properly when she was so mad.

Ninja woke up.

'What's the matter, Goth,' she asked, sensing the bad vibes straight away. 'You're scaring me.'

Goth looked at the child and stilled herself for two reasons. Drastic times called for drastic measures and Ninja had provided her with exactly what she needed.

*****

Mel was enjoying her holiday. La Manga was new to her and there was plenty to do in the resort whether or not she wanted to watch the weight lifting. She wasn't a big fan of the sport but adored her father so would watch everything in his weight class to show her support. She had meant to study but there was so much going on that all her plans had gone to rat shit. But that wasn't the only reason. She smiled to herself. Dean wasn't a weight lifter, he was visiting with his parents and his brother Lee who was in the competitions. They were all getting together with other members of their family who lived in Spain. Mel had got talking to Dean at one of the bars and they had hit it off instantly. They spent as much time together as they could, Dean trying his best not to neglect his family. Both were besotted and Mel had put her course work to one side so she could spend time with him. Her father Graham had progressed to the quarter-finals in the competition and so had Lee, Dean's brother. Thankfully they weren't competing against each other, Graham was in a lighter weight division so was performing first.

Dean's brother Ben arrived with his wife and two adorable daughters. The parents sat in the row in front and the sisters sat next to Dean. Mel noticed again that the older was very protective of the younger. It seemed more than the usual older sibling stuff and she decided she'd ask Dean about it when she remembered – they were usually too busy doing other things when they were alone in his room. Mel laughed out loud.

'What's funny?' asked Millie, the oldest.

'I was just thinking about something that happened before and it made me laugh,' Mel answered.

Millie thought her strange but Daisy wanted to know what it was.

'Umm, well...'

The clapping of the crowd distracted her. 'Mel's father is in the first competition,' said Ben.

'I hope he wins,' Daisy smiled shyly.

'Me too, Daisy.'

Graham and his fellow performers entered the performance area. Mel stood up and cheered when her father was introduced and Dean joined in along with his nieces.

*****

Goth watched the crowds gather in the hall, then the start of the competition.

'Daisy looks as if she's having fun,' she said. Ninja folded her arms and bit her bottom lip.

109

'It's not fair,'

'Who's she sitting with?' asked Goth. The girl in her late teens or twenties looked vaguely familiar but she couldn't place her. She wondered if she knew her or if she reminded her of anyone.

'That's my Uncle Dean and they're going to watch my Uncle Lee.'

'Oh look. Your uncle's tickling Daisy and she's giggling. Did you like to watch the shows?'

'Yes, and look at Daisy, she's not watching.'

'Would you like to go back to your body so you can watch from down there?'

'Can I?'

'Of course you can. Come on, I'll show you.'

Ninja followed Goth as they hovered above the audience in the hall. 'I want you to tell your family that you're back for a visit, and you want Daisy to leave your body. Do you understand?'

Ninja said she did. She wanted her body back anyway and perhaps she'd be allowed to stay there this time.

'If you really want your body back you can help them to like you more than Daisy, then they'll want you back.'

'How do I do that?'

'Do you remember when you used to live in your body and you used to be naughty? What did you used to do?'

'Like when I pulled Millie's hair and mum made me sit in the naughty chair and took my iPad from me.'

'That's right, Ninja.'

'And when I hit Lottie Pike with a ruler and she had a mark on her face. But it was only because she hit me first and Mrs Gray didn't see that and it wasn't really my fault.'

'It's not fair is it? We can deal with Mrs Gray another time.'

'It's okay. I don't want to do that.'

Goth hoped she hadn't gone too far. She needed to convince the child to cause chaos so they could pay back some of the humiliation of Sandy being kidnapped from the Devil.

'So do you want to get your own back on the girl who's in your body?'

Ninja looked down at Daisy again. She was cuddling into Uncle Dean and talking to the older girl that Ninja didn't know. She hated her more than Lottie Pike and Goth said if she did what she was told, she could have her body back.

'Yes.' Consumed with hate and jealousy, Ninja forgot her manners.

'Here's what I want you to do.'

*****

During the break in proceedings where the other performers left the stage, Ben and Polly asked whether Dean and Mel would look after the girls while they went for a look around.

'Okay with me,' said Dean. 'Mel?'

'Not a problem, they're no trouble at all.'

'See you in a bit.'

Graham was the first to perform in his class and he was preparing himself with his pre-lift routine.

Mel took a drink before turning her attention to the girls. She felt a shiver down her spine, then noticed a change in Daisy almost immediately. The gentle, shy child started talking non-stop, saying how much she loved watching the competitions and hoped her Uncle Lee was going to win. When she'd asked her about the competition a few minutes earlier, Daisy said she was looking forward to seeing it as it was her first. Every time Mel went to ask her a question she ignored her, but looked adoringly at her Uncle Dean and interrupted whenever Mel tried to speak to him. It was as if she'd become a completely different child. Her sister looked worried and had edged away from Daisy.

'Can I come and sit by you, Mel?' asked Daisy and Mel wondered what the hell was going on.

Daisy's constant chatter was driving her nuts. Her father was about to start lifting and she was still wittering on.

Mel watched as Daisy went to hold her uncle's hand with her left hand, and her right pulled it back and put it by her side. It was as if there was some sort of internal struggle going on.

Dean shrugged at Mel, looking as confused as she was. 'Are you all right, Daisy?' he asked.

As she answered, Graham approached the bar and the crowd clapped and cheered. They hadn't heard Daisy's reply and she was annoyed.

'My body and my uncle!' she shouted this time and people in the rows in front turned around to shush her.

Millie cringed, and looked to the left, hoping her parents would soon return. There was no sign of them as yet.

Daisy continued to chat incessantly and the people around them tutted and gave their group dirty looks.

Mel decided to try another tack. 'Please be quiet, Daisy,' she said. 'That's my father up there and I want to watch him. Look, so does everyone else.'

'And I want my Uncle Lee to win,' said Daisy. She got up and marched towards the stage. The two staff at the front were watching Graham with their backs turned to the audience. They hadn't noticed the young girl climbing onto the stage. Mel and Dean had no idea what Daisy intended to do, but moved as one when she approached Graham.

They were too late.

As Polly and Ben returned to the arena and made their way to their seats, they saw their daughter pick up a weight that should have been impossible for her to lift.

Graham was concentrating on the bar in front of him and had zoned out. As he lifted it his world went into slow motion. A child carrying a fifteen kilogram weight was running towards him. In the process of returning the bar to the floor he had nowhere to go when she dropped it on his foot. Dropping the bar he held he felt a crunch and an intense pain travelled from his foot, right up the rest of his body. He screamed in agony.

'I want Uncle Lee to win,' said Daisy before appearing to faint as she collapsed in front of Graham.

112

'Noooooo,' shouted Mel as she jumped onto the stage, ignoring Daisy and running to her father. One of the staff called the emergency services and it wasn't long before medics arrived to treat both Graham and Daisy.

'What an evil child,' Graham shouted. He was in agony and the medics gave him morphine for the pain, so he was out of it as soon as the drug started to kick in.

Polly and Ben rushed towards their youngest daughter. She was now fully conscious and looked stunned.

'What happened?' asked Daisy as she looked around at all the commotion.

'You attacked Mel's father,' said Dean.

'No I didn't,' Daisy replied. 'It was Ninja.'

Polly's hand flew to her mouth to stop herself from screaming and Ben put his arm around her, trying to comfort them both. Millie was still in the audience at the front of the stage. She cried quietly while looking at her family, wondering whether anything would ever be the same again.

Goth did little twirls as she watched from above. The child had exceeded her expectations making her happy in her own evil way. The balance was definitely changing in their favour and the Devil would recognise she was a major contributor.

She had no idea her sadistic joy would be short-lived as she made her way to retrieve young Ninja.

*****

Gabriella and the others returned Sandy to Cherussola. Ron was still in a deep sleep and Sandy was chuntering like a mad woman. Knowing she was badly damaged, they laid her down next to the soul she loved so she could have a long rest. Just like the others before her who had returned from Hell, they didn't know how broken she was, if she would recover, and if so, how long it would take. The junior angel who had nearly been caught was in a much worse state than Gabriella would have ordinarily expected. She decided she'd been too cavalier in selecting the souls and angels to accompany her on missions. Although they all had their own hang-ups, her brother and his soul mate seemed fearless so this had made Gabriella assume the courage and bravery of the others as a given; this mistake could have cost them to lose more than one of their own. She vowed to revise her selection process and decided to ask the advice of the Committee. It wouldn't hurt for her leaders to think she needed their wisdom and experience. She needed to select the right team and train them so they would be mission ready. But before any of that, they all needed some rest and recuperation.

Their sleep was interrupted by the news of Ninja's possession of Daisy. This upped the ante so when Gabriella was awoken she asked for a meeting with the Committee. She was pleased to see her mother back where she belonged, presiding over the others. Gabriella counted nine of them meaning her mother would have the deciding vote of any split decisions.

'What can we do for you?' asked Amanda.

She explained her predicament. 'This young soul they call Ninja has already been corrupted by one of the senior evils. I fear for her future if we don't rescue her soon. The mission is so important I want to ensure we only take those that are ready.' She went on to give feedback from the last mission.

They hummed and ahed while considering the way ahead.

*****

Mel's mum Carol was staying with her sister and her family while she recovered from her operation. Mel didn't want to worry her so phoned Marion. She told her what had happened.

'It was like there was another presence, Auntie Marion. I had the same feeling as when that nasty spider attacked me,' she sighed. 'It was really weird but it was like Dean's niece was possessed or something. When she woke up after fainting she was disorientated and I swear to God, she didn't know what she'd done.'

114

'So how's your father? I don't expect a young girl can do much damage?'

'Well that's where you're wrong. She managed to pick up a fifteen kilogram weight and drop it on his foot. It was crushed and they have to rebuild it.'

'There's something wrong with the line, Mel,' said Marion and she walked to another part of the room to get a better signal. 'It sounded like you said fifteen kilograms.'

'Yes! That's exactly what I said. She's only seven and small for her age but managed to run with the weight from one side of the stage to where dad was performing, lifted the weight to her chest then dropped it on his foot, saying she wanted her Uncle Lee to win the competition.'

'Oh my God how awful. Your father must have been in agony.' It had been a long time since Marion had wished for bad things to happen to her ex. She now felt sorry for him, knowing how much he loved his weight lifting, which had turned from a hobby to a serious sport.

'He's in hospital now but we're both travelling back home tomorrow. He's going to stay with mum at Auntie Sylvie's.'

'I see. Well if there's anything I can do to help, Mel. Just let me know.'

'Well actually...' she explained that her aunt only had one spare room and that Marion's house was nearer to where Dean lived.

Marion laughed. 'You're welcome to stay here and your boyfriend can stay over too if you want, but I'll need to speak to your mother about the umm,' Marion coughed and Mel could imagine her blushing.

Now it was her turn to laugh. 'Thanks, that's great. I'm almost twenty and I'm sure I'm not doing anything you didn't at my age, but if it makes you feel better to speak to mum...' Mel gave her the number.

Mel's directness reminded her again of Claire and she smiled, grateful once more for having a major role in the young girl's life.

'Dean needs to go home first,' Mel continued. 'His parents are upset about what happened with his niece. She's been taken into the local hospital for now to undergo all sorts of analysis Dean said. The family are trying to get the authorities to discharge her so they can bring her back to this country where she'll be near her grandparents for support.'

'That makes sense so when are you coming to me,' asked Marion.

'I'm flying home on Saturday with dad. His foot is in a cast so I'll drop him off with mum and make sure they're both all right before coming down to you. Dean's leaving with his family today and will come to yours on Sunday if that's all right and stay until mid week.'

They hung up shortly after and Marion was pleased that Mel wanted to stay with her, when the loved up couple could have had her own home to themselves while her parents were with Carol's sister. It would be company for her as Basil, the twins and their wives were all away doing one thing or another. Well that's what she thought until she got the first call.

'Hi Marion,' it was Fiona and she sounded rushed as usual. 'I thought it would be good to see you this weekend, are you free for me to come over?'

'Mel's here from Saturday and her new boyfriend arrives on Sunday, but feel free to join us.'

Fiona said that would be lovely and that she would arrive sometime on the Friday night.

'How are the boys?' Marion asked when Fiona arrived and was told they were busy as usual doing whatever it is they do.

'Other than that all's fine,' said Fiona.

'You didn't tell me that the twins work with Basil.'

Fiona spluttered her wine over the arm of the chair and Marion gave herself a mental pat on the back, knowing her suspicion had been confirmed. She'd caught her daughter-in-law off guard and could see Fiona was annoyed with herself. On the practical level Marion was glad her three-piece-suite was leather. She tried not to look smug as she left for the kitchen to get a damp cloth.

'You can tell me all about it,' she said on her way out.

Fiona had no intention of doing so and headed up to her bedroom as soon as Marion was in the kitchen.

When Violet saw who was calling, she answered on the second ring. Fiona quickly explained her faux pas.

'Hmmm,' her boss pondered for a moment. 'Basil did say it was hard to pull the wool over Marion's eyes. I'll have to speak to the Director.'

'But what do I tell her in the meantime? She wants to know more. She's going to be annoyed if I know the boys and Basil work together, but she doesn't.'

The plan was to try to recruit Marion and possibly Libby. Marion was too savvy to be kept out of the loop and if they wanted the whole family and Basil to relocate to Scotland, Libby would need to be included in the equation.

'Tell her you have signed the Official Secrets Act and that if you divulge any information, you will go to prison.'

'Seriously?'

'It's either that, Fi, or lie. And clearly that's not going to work with your mother-in-law. Don't let this distract you from getting the information we need, but do try to be subtle and talk to Mel when Marion's not there if possible.'

'Will do. I think I need another drink.'

'You and me both,' said Violet. 'But go easy and good luck.'

She turned to her husband after the call.

'Yes I heard,' he said. 'We need to talk, but first...'

*****

'Spill,' said Marion as Fiona returned to the living room.

'You're right, Marion. Jim told me they already knew Basil and they work for the same company, but that's as much as I know.'

x

117

'Seriously?' She wondered what Tony had told Libby but her other daughter-in-law wasn't there to ask. She decided to change the subject. 'And what are you really doing here this weekend? I don't usually have the pleasure of your company when Jim's away.'

Fiona fidgeted and Marion noticed her discomfort. 'So was Graham right? We all took the mickey when he told anyone who would listen that his boys were spies. But is that close to the truth?'

'I'm afraid I can't say anything further without breaking the Official Secrets Act that I have signed. You need to speak to your sons, Marion. I think under the circumstances maybe I should leave.'

Marion knew she'd opened a very big can of worms, but was excited her instincts had proved to be correct.

'There's no need to leave,' she said, knowing Fiona expected that response. 'We'll enjoy the weekend and nothing more will be said about this subject.'

Fiona smiled gratefully, glad the awkwardness was over but not knowing what would happen now the cat was out of the bag.

They had a girl's night in on the Saturday planning to watch a chic flick. That plan went out of the window as Mel was buzzing with information.

'Shall I put some music on?' asked Marion. Nobody was watching the movie so they all agreed.

'It was such a shock to see a child acting like that,' said Mel, regaling them with the whole story. She included every detail making Fiona glad and relieved she didn't have to pump her for information. Despite not discussing the job issue, Marion was watching her every move, which meant she was on her guard.

'It was really upsetting too. Dad was in agony. When I phoned the twins to tell them, Tony said he knew someone who'd had his foot crushed and that dad would be all right.'

So the twins already knew and that, thought Marion, is why Fiona is here to get more information out of Mel. But why?

'It's good to know there's not going to be any lasting damage,' said Marion. 'I hope he's able to get back into his competitions.' She meant every word. The bitterness she'd felt towards her ex had left and Marion was the happiest she'd been in years. She loved Mel as if she were her own and knew that if her parents were ill, it would make her unhappy. It therefore made sense that Marion wanted them both to have a speedy recovery so that Mel could concentrate on her studies and the relationship with her boyfriend.

They chatted for the rest of the night, Mel interjecting snippets of the very unusual attack on her father. It sounded to Marion as if the child had a complete personality change or was possessed. She reined in her imagination and decided to talk to Basil about it. Mental illness was his field of expertise after all and she wondered if he had come across any similar cases.

Dean arrived the following day and Marion and Fiona were charmed. He was attentive to Mel but was also aware she could sometimes be bossy. Another trait shared by Claire thought Marion. After getting three rounds of drinks and washing up the dishes that night, he put his foot down when Mel asked for some snacks.

'I'm all for impressing your family and friends, Mel, but you're taking the mickey now.'

She laughed. 'It was worth a try.' Mel got up to go to the kitchen and stopped to give him a kiss on the way.

'Get a room,' said Fiona.

'Actually, do you fancy watching a movie, upstairs?' she asked Dean.

He said he did and ten minutes later the sound of the film drowned out any other noises coming from their room.

When they had all left by the Wednesday morning, the apartment felt quiet and empty. Marion reflected on the time spent with her visitors. She was delighted to see Mel so happy with a young man she clearly loved and who adored her too. She was looking forward to seeing Basil the following weekend and trying to discover more information about his working relationship with the twins. *Official Secrets Act* my eye, thought Marion. Halfway upstairs to sort the bedding for the washing machine, the phone rang so she made her way back down. She didn't recognise the number and wondered if she should ignore it. Although her number wasn't public, she did sometimes receive calls from salesmen wanting to sell her windows or even worse, ambulance chasing companies. She let it ring and jogged up the stairs. Ten minutes later when the first wash was on and Marion was making herself a coffee, the phone rang again. It was the same number. Persistent buggers she thought as she picked it up, determined to give them a piece of her mind.

'Yes?' she said.

'Hello, Marion,' said the voice on the other end. 'My name is Violet Hennessey and I work with the twins, Basil and Fiona. I wondered if we could meet up somewhere for a chat?'

'What a good idea,' Marion replied.

The arrangements were made for that afternoon and by the time she left home, Marion was almost buzzing with excitement.

Chapter 12

Libby was excited about starting the new chapter in her life. Spike was coming home with her the following day and Tony would be home for the weekend, later. She was dying to see his reaction to the dog knowing he loved German Shepherds and had wanted one for ages. It had always been her who had put him off, saying their lives were too busy to look after a dog. And fair play to Tony, thought Libby, he had gone along with her wishes.

She slept well that night. Since working with Cassie and walking the dogs she had slept much better. She wasn't sure whether it was the act of unburdening her problems or the fresh air, it didn't matter which, the fact that it worked was enough.

Before leaving for the centre the following morning she checked that all was ready for Spike. Libby already loved the three month old puppy. He was bright and picked up anything he had to do very quickly. She knew the transition to home life would be an easy one for them both.

Cassie picked up on her excitement and so did the other animals.

'Fancy lunch before you go home,' said Cassie. 'Or do you want to go now and get him settled before your other half comes home?'

'We could go into town for lunch then come back and I'll collect Spike. No doubt Tony will be late again so there's plenty of time.'

It was the answer she'd wanted to hear and Cassie gave her a spontaneous hug. Libby felt something again so broke away, trying to ignore it. From the look on her face, Cassie had felt the same too.

'It's all right,' Cassie put a hand on Libby's arm. 'Let's go for lunch then get Spike's stuff together and pack your car when we return. He knows something's going on too, look at him.'

True enough the puppy was following Libby's every move, wagging his tail with enthusiasm.

He gave a big sigh and flopped down onto his bed as they said goodbye to him before leaving to have some lunch. The tension was still between them but neither wanted to cancel lunch and wait until the following Wednesday before seeing each other. Over their burgers they remembered how well they got along and the tension seemed to melt away.

Back at the centre Libby addressed the puppy.

'We're going home, Spikey, Wikey.'

Cassie rolled her eyes at Libby's baby talk. 'He's a dog not a baby, Libby for God's sake.'

'But he's my baby, oh yes he is,' she said, as she tickled Spike behind his ear. It was his favourite spot and he loved it. She put his lead on then led him to the car where he jumped up into his cage without any hesitation.

'He is a clever boy,' said Cassie. 'You've got a good one there.'

'I know and I can't thank you enough,' Libby smiled. 'A few months ago there was no light at the end of the tunnel but now I know I can be happy again. Thanks Cassie for bringing me back.' Libby wiped a tear from her eye.

'Think nothing of it.'

They hugged again before Libby said goodbye and quickly got into her car. Her emotions were all over the place and she didn't trust herself around Cassie any more. As she drove off she convinced herself it was just gratitude for all that Cassie had done for her that made her feel this way.

At home later that day she kept herself busy settling Spike in and cooking a meal for Tony. Every time thoughts of Cassie entered her head, she purposely pushed them aside and concentrated on the weekend ahead.

Spike gave a soft bark and sat by the front door. Ten minutes later Libby heard the key in the door. The puppy pounced on Tony, showering him with kisses.

'Hello and who do we have here?' Tony stroked and tickled the dog. It was love at first sight for them both.

'His name's Spike,' said Libby. 'I knew you'd love him.'

Although he'd calmed down, Spike was still demanding attention, but Tony told him to go and lie down and Spike obeyed.

'What do you mean?'

'I've been planning to surprise you for a few weeks. They usually prefer the family to visit before adopting but I just knew Spike would be perfect for us both. You've always wanted...'

'So despite the fact I work away and you are out of the house for a large part of each day, you've got us a dog without even talking to me about it?' He was trying not to raise his voice, but struggling.

'Don't you like him?'

She sounded like a five year old and Tony sighed. 'Of course I like him. If we'd discussed it and visited the Rehoming Centre together he would be the one I picked. I'm just a bit upset that you didn't discuss it with me first. Don't you get it?'

Libby nodded, saying she did, but no apology was forthcoming. 'I'll sort dinner,' she said.

'What did mum say? Is she happy to have a dog in her apartment when you're out during the week?'

Libby hesitated on her way to the kitchen. 'I've moved back home, Tony and told your mother I was moving out. She hasn't met Spike yet.'

'But when?...'

She didn't answer and he looked at his wife's back as she walked into the kitchen, feeling like he hardly knew her any more. She hadn't told him about the dog or about moving out of his mother's. He wondered if there was anything else she was keeping from him. Tony was lost in his own thoughts as Spike moved off his bed and crawled over to him. He laid his head on Tony's feet.

'Hello,' Tony said and soon found the sweet spot behind his ear. As he played with the puppy, he wondered if he'd been a little harsh with Libby. He could already see that Spike was a wonderful dog but he was still hurt for not having been involved in the decision to adopt him, or in her decision to move. He believed she still needed help but knew if he said something, she was likely to kick off.

Libby watched her husband and dog as she laid the table for dinner. Both oblivious to her, there was already an unbreakable bond between them.

She should have felt happy.

The weekend ended and Tony was relieved to say goodbye to his wife, but it was already a wrench for him to leave Spike. To make matters worse the puppy was morose after he left and Libby couldn't cheer him up, no matter how much she tried. She wasn't supposed to be working with Cassie until Wednesday but convinced herself that she needed to speak to her about Spike's strange behaviour, since Tony had left that morning. Cassie smiled as she ended the call and made her way into town to meet Libby for a coffee, eager to see her friend. As Libby left the house she felt guilty leaving Spike on his own and hoped he wouldn't make a mess or chew their belongings while she was out.

*****

There was no time to carry out the enhanced selection process before selecting souls and angels for the job of rescuing Ninja. Amanda discussed the issues with the Committee and they interviewed the potential candidates one by one, knowing that the souls who were inarticulate in front of the Committee, would likely be the wrong ones for the job due to their nervousness or lack of confidence. It wasn't perfect and they may have made mistakes, but it was the only way they could think of given the short notice. Amanda vowed not to be in the same situation in future so decided to ask God's permission to train angels for specific tasks. Gabriella's suggestion made perfect sense so she hoped it would enhance her standing in the eyes of their lord.

Ninja's rescue party consisted of all angels, most of them high grade who had already experienced rescue missions with Gabriella. They had all volunteered and knew there was a risk of being caught themselves, if the rescue went wrong. Claire and a few others were the most junior and although Claire felt honoured to be amongst this company, she knew she had earned her place.

In the past Goth-Roach had moved around a lot and only remained static when she was planning to send Ninja to possess Daisy. They hoped this was the case now as they left the safety of Cherussola and headed for the ether on the hunt for the young soul. It would be a bonus if Claire was allowed to deal with Goth-Roach and return her to the cave, but after a talking to from Gabriella, she knew that was unlikely. They had been told collectively to rescue Ninja quickly and to get out. They were not to get into any fights unless they were unavoidable. In addition, Gabriella had spoken to Raphael and Claire separately repeating what was required, so they were in no doubt.

Goth watched mesmerised as her Ninja, as she liked to think of her, possessed the soul of Daisy and caused havoc while Daisy was in an appointment with her psychiatrist. It wasn't the chaos Ninja was causing that amazed Goth, she was used to that by now, it was the fact she recognised the two men who entered the room to restrain the child.

'Well, well, well,' she said to herself. 'If it isn't Tweedle Dum and Tweedle Dee.' She'd caused problems for the twins before and had used them to try to lure their sister into her clutches. She had also used them to escape from their sister but preferred not to dwell on that. Ninja's grooming was almost complete. Goth started planning for the next time. She'd send Ninja to Daisy with specific instructions so the twins and their hated angel sister would learn how wide her web of influence could spread. But for now she knew the youngster would be shattered. It was the longest visit to her old body and the most Goth had asked her to do. As the medic administered the injection and Daisy passed out, Goth saw Ninja leave the body and force herself upwards. It was hard work for the child and this was when she was at her most vulnerable. Goth had become too complacent while busy planning her next evil deeds and had left any thought of protection a little late. She wasn't overly bothered because there had been no attempts to wrestle Daisy away from her.

The rescuing angels couldn't believe their luck. The child soul was returning from a possession and was plainly disorientated and exhausted. They wouldn't get any trouble from her and her dangerous mentor was further away than they were.

Gabriella issued orders like a general about to go into battle.

'Raphael and Claire, go and collect the soul. Be as gentle as you can and take her home as quickly as you can. Everyone else follow me. We're going to form a circle of love around Goth-Roach and stall her until she screams for reinforcements. Hold fast unless you're in extreme pain or in real danger of being taken to Hell. Everyone ready?'

Wings wiggled and flapped and all eyes were on Gabriella.

'Let's go.'

Claire would have given anything to be in the circle, to have a chance of fighting with Goth-Roach, but she guessed Gabriella knew that would make her the weak link. She had to put her own needs to the back burner, knowing there would be other times to deliver the evil her just desserts.

Goth heard the whoosh before she saw them. As she started to move so she could retrieve Ninja, the angels suddenly appeared all around her. She did a double take, wondering if she was imagining their circle and if not, how had they got there without her seeing them approach?

They closed in towards her and Goth knew she couldn't fight them all. What she could do was make their job harder so before making her attack, she screamed for help. Gabriella had expected the nasty bitch to start fighting first, then call for help. She knew the clock was ticking so hoped her brother and Claire would have enough time to rescue Ninja and take her far enough away from danger, before the evils gave up their chase. Goth looked around the circle and judged a male angel to be the weakest. She

126

attacked him first and though he was in pain, he didn't break the circle. The strength of her attack had forced the circle to move and, as it did, she saw two other angels below them in the distance, heading upwards. As they neared, Goth noticed the female angel was cradling Ninja in her arms. That and the fact she recognised it was Claire, made her incandescent with rage. Gabriella shook her head as Claire blew Goth-Roach a kiss on the way past and Raphael added to her fury by giving a little wave. Goth gave a loud, blood-curdling scream, which shook the atmosphere and woke Ninja. She saw her keeper in the circle of love and didn't understand why she was so upset.

'Where are we going?'

'On holiday to a warm and bright place,' said Claire.

'Will we see the sea?'

'If you want to, Ninja,' said Raphael. 'Wave goodbye to Goth now.'

'Bye bye, Goth,' she said as she waved.

'Hold tight,' shouted Gabriella knowing they would succeed in their mission, but some of her company would take a beating for that to happen.

Not much later the angels left Goth exhausted and beaten, just before the other evils arrived.

*****

Violet had arranged to meet Marion at the car park outside Dordsey Manor. She smiled as she saw the long, winding driveway leading up to the magnificent gardens, then the large building which had once been home to the Earl of Dordsey and his ancestors, remembering her last visit with Basil. Newly renovated, it now had many mod cons but still kept the traditional structure. It was popular for weddings and other big events but also a great location for those who loved the countryside.

When Marion had asked how she would recognise her, Violet had told her not to concern herself, but to be there for two o'clock. She was approached by a middle-aged woman who introduced herself as Violet.

127

'Good to meet you, Marion at long last. I've heard so much about you.'

'Have you now,' said Marion, as they shook hands.

'Shall we?'

'Where are we going?'

'I have a room booked where we can talk in private.'

Violet didn't ask if she was comfortable with this, so Marion hesitated for a moment. With Fiona referring to the Official Secrets Act and Marion not knowing this woman from Eve, she wondered if this could be some sort of set up.

Violet had anticipated her hesitation. She took her phone out of her pocket and made a call. 'I'm with Marion. Can you reassure her we're with the good guys and not going to do anything dodgy?'

Violet handed the phone over.

'Marion it's Basil.'

'We have some talking to do at the weekend,' she replied.

'I know, darling. I'm sorry but I've signed the...'

'That's what Fiona said too,' she cut him off. 'This had better be good, Basil.'

'Violet recruited me, Marion. You have nothing to worry about and it's safe to go with her. I'm glad you're going to be in on this. I was never comfortable keeping it from you.'

'I'll reserve judgement until I know more,' she looked at Violet. 'I'll see you on Friday evening.'

'You certainly will, Marion, love you.'

'I know, goodbye.'

She had no intention of arguing with him in front of someone she didn't know. But it was the first time she hadn't reciprocated when he said he loved her, so he would know how annoyed she was. She handed the phone back to Violet and followed her to the door.

Violet made small talk and Marion started to relax, feeling more comfortable with her. She realised the woman was probably trained to do this but it was still a pleasant experience.

128

'Martha Jones,' Violet said to the receptionist.

Marion noticed she didn't even flinch when handing over the credit card in the false name. Feeling like an extra in a Bourne movie, she wondered how many false identities Violet had assumed.

Violet signed the form and took the key card, then headed to the lift as the receptionist had directed. Marion followed in silence. As she had expected, it wasn't the standard double, but a suite. It wasn't the top of the range sumptuous one but the area had a bedroom with twin beds and a separate room with a comfortable-looking settee and a small dining table with two chairs. Violet put down her bags and removed what looked like a small metal rod from one of them. She pulled one end and the rod extended. She appeared to flick a switch on the device and a red light lit up. She walked around the suite, pointing the rod in all areas.

'You can't be too careful,' she said before smiling at Marion. 'All clear.'

Marion was bemused, now feeling even more like she was in a spy movie.

'Tea or coffee,' asked Violet.

I wish she would just get on with it. 'Tea would be great thanks, black with nothing.' She decided to play the game, determined not to show her impatience.

As the kettle boiled, Violet took a large laptop out of her bag and fired it up. She placed the drinks on the table and they both sat down. The decision to recruit Marion had been a difficult but a necessary one. Difficult because she could never know that her twins were in contact with their dead sister. For some reason unknown to any of them, Claire was only able to communicate with her brothers and if her mother found out, she would be understandably upset. Basil was unaware of the twins communications with their sister, and since they'd discovered his relationship with Marion, it had been decided that he should never find out either. They knew he wouldn't be able to keep that secret from the woman he loved. They had therefore had two meetings. Firstly with the twins to explain their intention, and the second one with the twins and Basil where reference to Claire and that part of their ability was kept from him. Ryan and Janine had been present at both meetings. Fiona hadn't but already knew the twins communicated with their sister. It had become the norm for her and Libby, who wouldn't dream of telling Marion. They'd agreed on the job offer and the training Marion would require, and also how much she was to be told.

'Can I start by telling you that your assumptions are correct,' said Violet. 'Your sons and Basil work for the same organisation, and so does Fiona.'

'I knew it,' she said. 'So their father was right all along.'

'Not quite, Marion, but he wasn't far off.'

'What exactly do they do?'

'Basil is head of our psychiatric department and Fiona works for me, carrying out the background checks prior to selecting new members of staff.'

'I see.' She didn't *see* at all, but waited for Violet to continue.

'You will have realised that our organisation is only known to those in the highest echelons of government and to our members of staff. National security deems that it stays this way.'

Marion raised her eyebrows. 'So why am I here, Violet. What do you want from me?'

'We wondered if you'd like to come and work for us?'

'You what?'

Marion hadn't expected that and Violet laughed at her reaction.

'But I don't even know what you all do or what I could possibly do there. Especially if you're all spies. I couldn't do anything like that, not at my age...'

She was chuntering so Violet interrupted. 'I can explain further, but before I do I have to tell you that everything we talk about from now on is classified and subject to the Official Secrets Act. I need you to sign this

130

form and if you divulge any of this information to personnel outside our organisation, you will be subject to prosecution.' She produced the form.

Marion read it and knew it was make or break time. She had worked for various organisations during her life, but never anything like this. She considered what Violet had said.

'So could I discuss this with Basil and the twins?'

'Yes,' said Violet. 'And Fiona.' She didn't mention Libby as they had not yet approached her. 'But only where privacy is guaranteed such as their homes or yours, where you are absolutely sure you can't be overheard.'

'So how do you know that our houses are safe?'

Violet leaned back in her chair and smiled, realising that Marion was more perceptive than they gave her credit for.

'You might not be happy with the answer, Marion but...'

'So all the time I thought my boys were going about their business, completely safe in the offices of Arbuthnot and Lee, they were actually special agents doing God only knows what!'

'Not quite, but if you'll sign the form I can explain further.'

'And you had my home checked for bugs when I was out? Unbelievable.'

'We have a duty to ensure all our employees are as safe as they can be, within the parameters of their employment. That does mean we sometimes keep an eye out for their family and close friends and others they come into contact with. You can't be too careful these days.' She saw the look on Marion's face and quickly added. 'We have not been listening to your conversations, Marion but have ensured that nobody else does either.'

It was the invasion of privacy that annoyed her and Violet's words didn't make her feel any better.

'I can leave you to think about this if you wish or we can terminate the meeting here and now and you'll never hear from me again.'

They both knew that wasn't going to happen.

'Or you can sign the form and assure me you will only talk about this as we have discussed.'

Marion thought about her options. 'Can I speak to Jim or Tony? That's if they're not out chasing baddies.'

Violet laughed at the analogy. 'Of course, they're at our headquarters today.' She made a call and asked the person on the other end to get Jim or Tony to call back. Tony called within a few minutes and she passed the phone to Marion.

'Hello, mum, how are...'

Marion interrupted. 'What is it you do, Tony that makes these people think there's a need to watch my home? Do you and your brother work together? Are you spies and what sort of danger are you in?'

'Take a drink of water, mum. Then maybe I'll be able to get a word in.'

She could hear the smile in his voice and wasn't amused. 'This isn't a laughing matter.'

'I know it isn't but give me a chance to answer your questions.'

'Go on.'

'I can't tell you everything but we mostly work undercover so if we catch any, err, criminals for example, we might be disguised so they won't recognise us. And yes, Jim and I generally work together as part of a team.'

'What...'

'No we're not spies and everyone's job has an element of danger. Remember that office worker who was killed by a tree on his way home from work a few weeks ago? Well I bet he didn't think his commute was dangerous.'

'I don't think you can use that as an example. Why didn't you tell me any of this?'

'Because of national security, mum and I've already told you too much.'

132

'And how would you and your brother feel if I worked for your organisation?'

'We've already discussed it and we both think it's a good idea. What are you going to do?'

'I'm going to sign the paper and see what Violet has to offer.'

'That's great, mum. I'll see you at the weekend, but Libby might not be with me, depending on what's going on at the centre.'

'Bye, son. Love you.' Now wasn't the time to discuss her concerns about her son and his wife.

'You too, mum. Bye.'

Marion passed the phone back to Violet and read the piece of paper before signing and dating it at the bottom of the sheet. 'Right, what's so secret about your organisation?'

Violet loaded a video on her computer. 'Watch this first,' she said as she pressed the play button.

The image on the screen was one of a beautiful valley, surrounded by rolling rugged hills and countryside.

'Welcome to the School for People With Special Abilities,' said the narrator in BBC English. The camera then panned from the valley to a large building that was surrounded by barbed wire, then high fencing. CCTV cameras were affixed to a number of the walls.

Violet pressed the pause button. 'We call it SAPs,' she said. 'It's in an isolated location in the Scottish Highlands and the public are led to believe it's a high security facility and treatment centre for the most dangerous criminally insane members of society. We've recently expanded and one of the wings could actually be used for that purpose.' She pressed play again.

Marion looked at the screen and could understand why people would believe the lie when she saw the guards patrolling with their fierce looking dogs, and the barbed wire and fencing.

The narrator continued. 'The school has three wings. *A Wing* comprises talented individuals who are recruited from the public, plus members of the military. They are trained as undercover agents in the fight against enemies or potential enemies of the State, and the most dangerous criminal elements of society.'

'Some of the students in *B Wing* are also undercover agents. In addition these people are recruited for their more unusual talents, including telepathy and claims of psychic abilities. We are constantly running tests to validate these claims.'

'*C Wing* has been added recently, and is where patients with interesting conditions are brought when other facilities have found them untreatable.'

Marion pressed the pause button. 'I don't like the sound of C Wing,' she said. 'In which wing were my twins trained?'

'*B,*' said Violet.

'Yes, I knew it,' Marion sounded smug. 'It's their twin telepathy isn't it?' she didn't wait for Violet to answer. 'They've always had it which isn't unusual for twins but you probably already know that. What was unusual was they were also tuned in with their sister and it was almost as if they could all read each other's minds.' She was on a roll now and Violet listened quietly. 'It's from my side of the family not Graham's, my mother said my grandmother had second sight, and my great grandmother, but I didn't meet either of them. My mother was convinced they could speak to the dead too.'

'Really?'

'Yes, but she didn't give any examples and I wasn't interested in anything like that until Claire... until my daughter died...'

Violet saw the pain on her face. 'Are you all right?'

'I'm fine. They say that time heals but it doesn't. You learn how to deal with it but the pain is always there. Do you know about Claire?''

'Yes, Marion. When we did the family checks we discovered what happened to Claire. I'm so sorry.'

'Thank you. Shall we carry on?'

They watched the remainder of the video in silence.

'I'm amazed that this could be kept from the public for so long,' Marion shook her head. 'What job were you thinking of offering me?'

'We want to offer you an admin role, but with a difference. There's a load of administration for each person who comes to the school. Booking in, accommodation, issuing kit and equipment, writing their training programmes etc. Two receptionists have left recently so we have vacancies. We would like to offer you one of the jobs but we would also expect you to evaluate certain candidates. Students are often more relaxed with the admin staff than with those they think are assessing them, so may ask for your feedback or opinions. We would also expect you to come forward regarding any concerns. You are good with people, Marion, and have the emotional intelligence we admire at the school. What do you think?'

'I thought I was going to be offered something a bit, err, sexier.'

Violet laughed again. 'Well I'm sorry to disappoint you. We couldn't offer you anything in the Operations Centre as your sons are undercover agents, so the school policy prevents it. However, if you decide to take the job and want more of a challenge later, there is the possibility of a move to work for Basil in *C Wing*. You can discuss that with him at a later date.' Violet knew Basil wouldn't want that due to the dangerous nature of some of the younger new arrivals.

'It would mean locating to Scotland. I liked Edinburgh when I visited but don't know this area.'

'The teaching part of the school works on a term basis, Marion, and our admin staff work week on week off. Accommodation is provided in the school so you could commute if you wished or your family could relocate.'

Marion was trying to work it all out. She was ready for a new challenge but would need to think about it. If they moved to Scotland it would probably be easier for Basil, the twins and Fiona. But what would they tell Libby and what

135

about Mel? If the terms were the same as Mel's university terms, they could still see each other during her holidays.

'I think we could make this work. My main concern would be Libby, she's Tony's wife. You already know that right?'

Violet said she did. 'We are considering a role for Libby too, Marion...'

'Is that wise, considering her... well what I mean is she had some mental health issues.'

'Absolutely right, so we wouldn't want to put her in a situation of undue stress. Like any government department, secret or otherwise, we have a budget to work to and our accountants are always trying to find creative ways of giving staff what they need, but also to save money. Libby will be offered a job within this department. There are different levels of security clearance, depending where one is employed and their knowledge of our operating procedures. So Libby will be offered a job there so at least you could discuss basics as a family, but not detailed information in front of her.'

'If I decline your job offer?' asked Marion.

'Libby's position is dependent on what you decide, Marion. It's unlikely you would be on our radar if your sons and Basil weren't working for us. But as they are, we believe it would be easier for your whole family if you were also part of our organisation,' she smiled. 'The fact that you have skills and experience that will benefit the school is a bonus.'

Marion had already made her decision. Violet knew what the answer was going to be, but didn't want to alienate her by appearing smug or arrogant.

'You don't need to decide now. Think it over for a few days if you wish, then give me a call.'

Now it was Marion's turn to laugh. 'We both know I'm going to take the job, Violet. I look forward to working for you,' she offered her hand and they shook.

'Fantastic, Marion. Do you want to go home now or do you fancy a walk followed by dinner? We could discuss the practicalities of moving or staying and I can share my experiences?'

'That sounds perfect.' They left the room and headed outside. 'I'd like to give the news to Basil and the twins and Fiona of course when we're next together. Can I ask that you don't tell them before then?'

'Of course. I'd like to be a fly on the wall at that conversation.' Violet already liked Marion and knew they were going to be friends.

Chapter 13

Friday had come around again and Libby decided to go to the Rehoming Centre to meet up with Cassie and walk the dogs. She couldn't take Spike with her as she'd been told it could confuse or upset him if he thought he might be returning to the Centre.

She heard raised voices as she opened the door to the kennel area. Maddie and Cassie were shouting at each other.

'So you're accusing me of stealing some of the funds donated by the public because the books don't add up?' said Cassie.

'That's not what I said, Cassie, but you have to admit...'

'I admit nothing. You've been trying to get rid of me since you took on this business but now you're trying to tarnish my good reputation too. Well you can forget it. You're a conniving bitch and I quit.' She walked through to reception and slammed the door behind her.

'Cassie would never steal from you,' said Libby. 'She loves this job and is the most honest person I've ever met.'

'Oh please,' Maddie rolled her eyes. 'Don't tell me she's conned you as well. Libby you must realise...'

'The only thing I realise is that you're wrong and I would advise Cassie to sue for harassment and defamation of character.'

'She won't do that, Libby. You'll see the truth when the police charge her.'

'I know you're bluffing. You've never liked Cassie and when all this comes out in the open, you'll have egg on your face and be forced to apologise for your mistake. I can't work for someone like you. I quit.' She followed Cassie out of the door.

Maddie looked at the two other staff who had heard everything. 'Do you believe this?' she asked. They both raised their eyebrows then carried on with their work.

Libby had never seen Cassie so upset, understandably.

'We've never liked each other but I can't believe she would want to ruin my reputation by accusing me of dishonesty. What's wrong with the woman?'

Libby put an arm around her friend's shoulder. 'Anyone who knows you knows you're not capable of that, Cassie. You should sue her for harassment and slander.'

'What, and use all of my savings on a case I might not win.'

'But...'

'It's not only that. These things can take months, even years, and can be so emotionally draining. Is it worth the hassle?'

'It's your reputation though? It's just so unfair.'

They walked in silence for a while with Cassie trying to regain her composure.

'Life is unfair,' she said after a while. 'But I refuse to be a victim.'

'That's more like the Cassie we all know and love.'

Cassie knew she had to get away. She didn't want to think about what else could be uncovered if Maddie did contact the police. Although she'd covered her tracks well and used different pseudonyms, there was a chance she could be linked to other businesses. She took Libby's hand from around her shoulder and held it in her own. They stopped walking.

'Libby, I need to get away from here and not worry about anything for a while.'

'Oh. Where will you go?' She tried to hide her disappointment.

'Portugal. I went on a few trips there when I was in uni and got my boat licence. We could get away from it all and hire a boat for a while.'

'We?' Libby was trying to process the information.

'Yes we, Libby. Come with me, I know you'd love it.'

'But what about Spike, and Tony? I love them.'

'Do you realise you put Spike before Tony then? And it wouldn't be forever, unless you wanted it to be.'

'I don't know, Cassie. I...'

'I realise I've sprung this on you but I've been thinking of a change for a while to be honest. I'm sorry, I'm being unfair.'

'No it's not that,' she sighed. 'You know I haven't been happy for a while. Let me think about it and I'll talk to Tony this weekend.'

That's exactly what Cassie didn't want to happen, knowing that Libby's husband would try to talk her out of it. She had to trust her friend so couldn't share her thoughts.

'Okay. I'm going to look up the flights this weekend and will book on Monday. Phone me when you've made your decision.'

'Will do. Will you be okay on your own until then?'

'You're not my only friend you know,' Cassie laughed. 'Tomorrow I'm meeting two friends I flat shared with, so I'll be fine.'

Libby believed the lie and they went their separate ways.

*****

The Committee had already had two meetings in Cherussola, to discuss the way forward for Ninja. She was one of the poor young souls who had been taken mistakenly, before her time. Ordinarily she would have moved on to one place or another, or returned to Earth in another life, but it was more complicated. As an angel had made the mistake, they wanted to put it right and the consensus was that Ninja should be returned to her own body and given the chance of a full life. The complication arose with what they should do with Val's soul and how they should remove her from Ninja's body without the knowledge of the family. The child would have to die for the task to be carried out. The family had already been through enough trauma so it was a dilemma. Until Gabriella came up with the idea.

The Committee agreed and Claire was despatched to speak with her brothers.

Libby was waiting for Tony to come home, wondering how she would broach the subject of going away with Cassie for a while. Tony hadn't met her new friend though she had occasionally spoken about her. When he'd asked when they were likely to meet, she had always put it off. She wanted this part of her life exclusively for herself, and didn't want to risk Tony picking up on the vibes between her and Cassie.

Spike barked and went to the window. He wagged his tail before sitting down and looking outside. He appeared to be waiting for something. Libby thought it even stranger when about fifteen minutes later, he got up and headed for the front door. A few seconds later she heard the car and the dog barked excitedly. Tony was hardly through the door when Spike was all over him.

'Well hello, boy. I've missed you too.'

They loved each other and Libby was surprised to feel jealous. 'Remember me?' she said.

Tony felt the atmosphere straight away and his shoulders tensed. He forced a smile. 'Hi, love. What sort of a week have you had then?'

Well my best friend has asked me to go away with her for a while and I think it's a good idea.

'Oh you know,' she said. 'Same old, same old.'

They went through the motions of hugging and Tony attempted a proper kiss, but Libby turned her face so it was a peck on the cheek. *So that's how it's going to be this weekend* he thought.

'I thought we might go into town for a meal tonight, for a change?'

'I've got a better idea,' said Tony. 'Why don't we go down the pub, then we can take this one with us?' Spike barked when Tony looked at him and he petted the dog. 'Then we can get a takeaway and watch a movie when we get home. A chic flick if you like?' He knew it was a bit of compromise so had suggested a movie that Libby would like in the hope they could cuddle up on the sofa to try to regain some of their former intimacy.

'Okay,' she agreed knowing it wouldn't be the ideal place to talk but was better than the stilted atmosphere of the house.

Tony tried again during the short walk to the pub. 'How are you, Libby? Really?'

She ignored the question. 'Oh, I forgot to tell you earlier. Spike knew when you were coming home.' She explained the puppy's behaviour.

'I knew he was a clever boy.'

Spike barked on cue and they both laughed.

Libby was relieved her delaying tactics had worked and decided to get a quiet booth in the pub and speak to Tony then.

It didn't happen.

Other customers were there with their pets in the dog friendly pub. One older couple had an adult German Shepherd with them, so decided to join them and give advice on the best way to rear their dog.

'There's also a German Shepherd Club in the town,' said the woman. She explained how to get there and the activities that took place. 'It would be a great place to socialise your puppy,' she said. 'And to meet people with similar interests.'

Libby said she would look into it but the woman wouldn't leave it at that.

'I can pick you up next Wednesday evening if you like?'

'Ah, sorry, I can't make next Wednesday, I'm busy.'

'What you up to, Lib?' asked Tony.

She gave him a warning look. 'I'm out with Cassie on a work do. It was meant to be tomorrow but was postponed. Maybe the following week though.' It suddenly hit her that she wouldn't be there the following week. She was going to go away with Cassie so now there was just the simple matter of telling her husband. They eventually made their excuses and left the pub for home, via the Chinese takeaway.

Watching the film later, Libby couldn't bring herself to tell Tony her news so decided to put it off until the following day. They went to bed and she lay awake late into the night, excited about leaving but wondering how to tell Tony.

Pottering around the house the following morning, her phone rang while Tony was out with Spike.

'It's me,' said Cassie. 'I've found some flights leaving from Stansted tomorrow afternoon. It's make or break time, Libby.'

'I've decided to come with you but I haven't told Tony yet.'

Neither could hide their excitement as they chatted about their adventure. When she put down the phone, Libby didn't consider she was being unfair to Tony. This was the only way if they wanted their marriage to work in the long-term.

He came in whistling then smiled at her. 'Put on your glad rags tonight, Libby. We're having dinner in that restaurant you wanted to go last night.'

'Great.'

'We're meeting Jim and Fiona there at seven thirty.'

'Oh. I thought you meant on our own.'

He tried to stay upbeat even though it was obvious she wasn't happy. 'I know it's been ages since you and Fi had a catch up. You used to love going out with them as much as I did.'

'You just don't get it do you? Nothing's the same since mum died and I'm trying my best to deal with it. It's changed everything for me and...' she shook her head and looked down, not knowing what else to say.

'I know and I'm trying my best to deal with it too, and to look after you. But I can't seem to do anything right.'

'Perhaps we need some time away from each other?'

'Do you really think that's the answer, Libby? We're only together at weekends as it is.'

'Well perhaps...' he'd given her an opening but she still found it difficult to tell him she was going away.

Tony's phone rang.

'You'd better answer that, it's your mother.' They could both tell from the ring tone.

'I'll call her back, Libby, this is more important.'

'Answer it. There's nothing else to say.' She walked out of the room and he heard her run upstairs as he answered his phone.

'Yes, mum,' he said more sharply than he'd intended.

'Are you all right, son?'

'Sorry, mum. Not really, but nothing to worry about.' They chatted for a few minutes, Marion wondering when her son was going to tell her what was wrong, Tony determined not to share his marriage problems with his mother.

'We're meeting up with Jim and Fiona tonight and won't be coming over tomorrow. We've decided to have a quiet day instead. Are you free next weekend for a get together?' he asked.

She said she was and they finished the call. Marion was frustrated. Some sort of emergency had come up and Basil had to work that weekend and now she wouldn't see her sons and their wives. She would have to wait another week to tell them about her job. She wondered how she could do this without involving Libby. Hopefully, Violet would have spoken to her by then. She berated herself for being selfish wondering, for the first time, if Tony and Libby's marriage would survive for much longer.

Despite their earlier discussion, they had a good time with Jim and Fiona, but mostly thought Tony because the girls hadn't seen each other for ages and had a lot to catch up on. He heard snatches of their conversation and hid his surprise at how much Libby talked about her new friend Cassie and the time she spent with her. Jim noticed and gave him a questioning look. *I'll tell you all about it on Monday* he thought. Jim nodded in understanding.

144

When they got home later, neither had the appetite for another argument. They went to bed shortly after and Tony was surprised when Libby started kissing and caressing him. Their lovemaking wasn't as it used to be but she had made the first move and that gave him some hope for their marriage.

'Shall we all go for a walk this morning?' he asked.

Libby said she wasn't in the mood. 'But no need to rush back, I've got plenty to keep me busy.'

His dark thoughts diminished with every few steps he took and Spike was a great distraction from his problems at home. With him working away, Tony was amazed they had developed such a strong bond in so short a time. Two hours later he returned home energized.

Spike knew straight away that Libby wasn't there but it didn't click with Tony until he saw a piece of paper with his name on it, on the breakfast bar. He knew before he read it.

He was furious, then upset when he calmed down. He re-read the note three times before it fully sunk in. She was going away with her friend Cassie in the hope it would save their marriage.

'How the fuck is going away going to save our marriage?' he asked Spike. The dog put his head to one side as if he knew what Tony was talking about. 'And she hasn't said how long she's away for, only that I shouldn't try to contact her'. Tony sat down and put his head in his hands. His dog pawed his knee and cried. Tony lifted him onto his lap and cuddled him. They both cried together.

Spike stopped first, then Tony. He lifted the puppy up and held him in front of him. 'I've got to go to work tomorrow, fella, so what are we going to do with you? Eh?'

Spike barked on cue. Tony laughed so he barked again. 'Shall we phone my mother to see if she can look after you?'

Marion hadn't expected to hear from her son until later in the week. She knew it wasn't good news.

'What's happened?'

'Libby's gone away with her friend from the Dog Centre, mum.'

'I was going to say that a trip away will do her some good, but it doesn't sound like you think so.'

'She didn't talk to me about it, just left when I was out. She hasn't said where she's going or how long she's going to be away.'

'I take it you've tried phoning Tony?'

'Yes, of course,' he snapped. 'Sorry, mum. It's just that it's upsetting,' he stroked Spike to calm himself. 'She left me a short note telling me not to contact her, saying she'd be in touch when she's ready to come home. She also said she's doing this to save our marriage for God's sake!' Even though he was distraught, he knew better than to use any stronger language when talking to his mother.

'I'm sorry, son. I knew what happened to Val knocked her for six, but I didn't see this coming.'

'Me neither, mum. What am I going to do?'

'I think you need to give her some space. Give it a few weeks and perhaps she'll see sense and contact you.'

'You're right. But what if she doesn't? What if this is it and she's gone for good?'

'I'm sure she'll come to her senses, Tony.' Marion wasn't sure of anything but didn't want to make her son feel any worse. 'What are you going to do about your dog and work?'

'I don't suppose you'll...'

'Of course I will. From what you say he's well behaved. Can he be left on his own for a while during the day?'

They discussed the arrangements for Spike, and Tony was glad to talk about something other than his marriage and wife for a few minutes. His mother invited him over but he decided to spend the rest of the day alone.

'I'll tell Jim what's going on, and send an email to Carl because of the time difference.' Libby's brother had moved to Australia but Tony wanted him to be aware of what his sister was up to.

146

'Okay. Are you sure you'll be all right on your own?'

'I'm fine, mum. Now I come to think about it I'm more annoyed than anything else at the way she's done it.'

'I understand. Well take care and I'll see you when you drop Spike off tomorrow. But if you change your mind or need anything, call me.'

*****

It was Thursday morning and Libby had been gone for under a week. Tony hadn't heard from her and was sitting at his desk in his room in the school, reading about the many cases marked as possible child possessions. The atmosphere changed and he sensed his sister's presence.

'It's been a while,' he said.

'Sorry, been busy.'

'Because of all the possessed children?'

'Err, no,' said Claire. 'Just one particular case. Is Jim about I need to speak to you both?'

'Just a minute.'

Claire waited, but Tony didn't move. 'Please, Tony, I haven't got much time.'

'Don't worry,' as Tony replied his brother walked through the door.

'Hello, Claire,' said Jim. 'Are you suitably impressed?'

'Very,' she said laughing. 'So you guys don't even need mobile phones now?'

'I wouldn't go that far,' said Tony. 'Working with Professor Robert has taught us how to hone our telepathic skills. You know we've always been tuned into each other, well practice makes perfect. It takes a lost of concentration though, Claire, and is really tiring.'

'So today's show was just to impress me?'

'It worked didn't it,' said Jim. 'To what do we owe the pleasure of your company?'

'I want to talk to you about the child named Daisy.'

'She was one of the few that Basil couldn't do anything with. He genuinely believed she was possessed and although he's not religious, the only thing he could suggest

147

was an exorcism. Since she almost died in a drowning accident, Daisy's family say it's almost as if she's a different person. It's all very weird.' Tony explained.

They were quiet for a moment, as Claire registered the information from her brothers, so she could understand how the professionals felt about Daisy. Jim broke her concentration.

'By the way we have some good news and bad news. Did you know that Basil and mum are really serious about each other? I wouldn't be surprised if he proposes.'

'That's fantastic,' said Claire. 'If anyone deserves a second chance at happiness it's mum. Do you approve?'

'He's mad about her, Claire and treats her well. Mum's got a spring in her step that we haven't seen for ages.'

'Brilliant. I'll pay them a visit next time.'

'There's something else you need to know too,' Jim said. 'Mum's been offered a job here. It will be much easier if she says yes as she caught Fiona out so knows we all work together, including her boyfriend.'

'But mum can't work with you. She'll be devastated if she discovers I speak to you but not her.'

'Don't worry, Claire, that's all sorted. Neither mum nor Basil for that matter know about you, and that's the way it's going to stay. Mum will be told our telepathic abilities are being tested which is actually true and Basil already knows that.' said Tony.

'We'd probably move up to Scotland,' added Jim.

'Big changes for you all if that's what you decide. How do the girls feel about it?'

'That's where the bad news comes in,' said Tony.

'But I thought you considered mum working with you guys to be the bad news.'

They both laughed. 'Not at all,' said Jim.

Claire looked from one to the other. 'Is it Libby?'

'It certainly is,' said Tony, knowing there was no easy way of saying it. 'She's done a runner. Said she needed some space if we wanted our marriage to survive, so has gone off to God only knows where, with her new best friend.'

Claire resisted the urge to say that God was too busy to keep up with Libby's comings and goings.

'So my visit didn't do that much good then?'

'It did make her feel better, Claire, but she was restless and needed something new I take it. She's switched off her phone and that's it as far as I'm concerned. If she does decide to come back I'm divorcing her.'

'Seriously?' Jim and Claire said in unison.

'Yup. I've only just decided. The woman I fell in love with has been replaced with one I no longer know. What happened to Val was awful, and I tried my best. But I now know she doesn't give a shit about me so I need to move on.'

'I'm so sorry, Tony.'

'And me,' said Tony. 'If you happen to come across her on your travels, perhaps you can tell her we're through?'

Claire laughed, even though she knew her brother was only half joking. 'If I see Libby it'll be for all the wrong reasons, so you don't want to wish that on her. So are you all going to move to Scotland?' Claire asked, eager to change the subject.

Jim said Fiona loved Edinburgh so would be happy to move and Tony wanted a new start.

'What about mum and Mel?' asked Claire. 'I thought they were pretty close these days.'

Tony explained that Mel was in uni so they didn't see so much of each other anyway. 'It would be a good place for her to visit. And while we're on the subject of Mel, that brings me back to the subject of Daisy. Mel's boyfriend is her uncle.'

'It certainly is a small world,' said Claire. 'There are some issues with Daisy that I need your help with, but it's complicated.'

The twins waited.

'Basil's assumption is correct. The child is possessed.'

'I think you mean *was,* Claire. She's been fine for the last two weeks, no signs at all,' said Jim.

'In fact, she's going to be discharged tomorrow,' Tony added.

'No, that can't happen.'

'Why, Claire? What's wrong?'

'The child you see now is actually possessed. It's the wilder one that is the real Daisy. I need your help to rid the child of her invader so the possessions stop, once and for all.' Claire was under strict orders not to tell her brothers about Zach's mistake and she couldn't mention the fact that Val's soul was in the child's body. Certain information was never to be divulged to those on the living plane, although they were free to imagine whatever took their fancy. She'd been told to use whatever means she could to engage the assistance of her brothers. If she failed, it meant Ninja would have to go elsewhere or move on. It could also mean years of doubt and questions for Ninja's parents and sister.

'What do you want us to do?'

Claire explained. It was a massive request and the twins were stunned into silence.

'And what if we refuse?'

'If you refuse we will need to find other ways to achieve our aim. As I'm sure you appreciate, it could be more dangerous and painful for the child without your assistance.'

The alternative was unthinkable so the twins reluctantly agreed to help. They would have to convince Basil that Daisy was still possessed, so she wasn't discharged. They would need to act soon after this before Basil could carry out further tests and examinations. The siblings said their goodbyes and the twins formulated their plan.

Claire returned to Cherussola where Ninja was still sleeping. Gabriella knew it wasn't going to be an easy task and was aware of potential dangers from Goth-Roach and other evils, even before they attempted to return Ninja and extract Val. She picked the same angels as she had for the rescue job. They were on their way shortly after.

*****

150

Later that evening, while Basil was about to pack up to leave, the twins called in to see him. 'Our sister Mel asked if we could give Daisy a present from her uncle,' Tony said.

Basil couldn't see any harm in it. The child had seen the twins before and, like most youngsters, was fascinated by identical twins.

'Not a problem, I'll buzz you in,' he said, deciding to catch up on some paperwork while they visited Daisy.

He watched the corridor CCTV as the brothers joked with each other before entering Daisy's room. Less than five minutes later a noise alerted Basil and he looked at the CCTV again. The twins hurried out of Daisy's room and leant against the wall. Jim was holding his face. When he took his hand away, Basil could just see a lump starting to appear.

'What the hell,' he thought as he rushed to the secure door to meet them.

'What...'

'She's still possessed,' said Tony. 'And has the strength of a maniac.'

'You can't release that child into society,' Jim added.

Basil noticed Jim's eye was starting to close and knew he'd have a proper shiner. He approached the door but Tony put a hand on his arm. 'I wouldn't, Basil. She needs to be sedated. We'll go there now. What are you going to tell her parents?'

Basil knew this would be a major set-back for Daisy's family. He also knew he'd need to speak to them that evening to tell them about the attack. Their daughter would have to remain in the facility for the immediate future. Visitors weren't allowed and they assumed their child was still in the secure unit in Hertfordshire, where only weekly visits were permitted for those considered criminally insane, even children.

'Okay. Tell the nurses what's happened and that I'll write the prescription shortly. We need to sedate her quickly so she's not distressed. God knows what's going on in her head. Jim, see if they can give you the once over while you're there too, that looks painful.'

'It is but I'm fine.'

They made their way to see the medics, it was no coincidence that it was during the shift changeover and the nurses were very busy, updating the night shift of the day's happenings. Jim waited, chatting to one nurse as she got together the items she needed. Tony kept the others busy so they didn't see what the first nurse was doing. They quickly hurried to Daisy's room.

'I haven't done anything,' said Daisy, obviously distressed. 'One of them hit the other one.'

The nurse looked at the twins. 'Poor child is delusional as well. Not surprising really, considering all she's been through.'

'It's okay, Daisy. Everything's going to be okay.'

Daisy struggled so the twins held her while the nurse administered the injection. 'I'll wait to make sure there's no reaction.'

'That's okay,' said Tony. 'You get off, we'll stay and will contact the medics if there's any problems.'

It had been a long day so the nurse took them up on their kind offer. Daisy hadn't had any adverse reactions to the drugs before, so there was no reason to expect any different now.

'That's good of you, especially after that,' she nodded towards Jim's face. 'You need to get it seen to.'

'I'm fine,' he insisted, so she said her goodbyes and left them to it.

As soon as she left the room, Tony removed the syringe and drug from his pocket. Jim leaned against the door as his brother emptied the syringe into Daisy's arm. 'Christ I hope we're doing the right thing,' he said, knowing there was potential for disaster.

Daisy's pulse weakened then stopped altogether. Tony opened Daisy's eyes, which looked dead to him. Her skin was already starting to feel cold.

'Claire, now's the time,' said Jim, but neither sensed her presence.

'Come on.' Tony muttered, willing and silently praying for his sister to make an appearance.

*****

Claire and Raphael watched as Gabriella woke Ninja up. She was still groggy but smiled at the beautiful black angel.

'You're going back to your body,' said Gabriella as she stroked her hair. 'But this time you're going to stay there and you won't remember anything about us, or Goth.'

Ninja returned Gabriella's smile. 'I like it here. I want to stay with you.'

The angels were used to being adored so none were surprised. 'I know you do, but it's not your time. Come on, I'll come with you.' Gabriella took her hand as they made their way downwards. As they did so, the bemused soul of Val that had occupied Daisy's body floated passed them. 'Look after her,' Gabriella called before disappearing.

*****

'Come on, wee lassie,' said Tony.

'You've gone all native and we haven't even relocated yet.' Neither laughed at Jim's attempt to lighten the situation. If Claire's plan didn't work they would be child murderers and would struggle with their consciences as well as the possibility of ending up in jail.

The atmosphere changed and the twins sensed the presence shortly after.

'Claire?' said Tony but Jim shook his head. They both knew it wasn't their sister. They waited a few moments but no signs were forthcoming. Less than a minute later Daisy groaned then turned over onto her other side. Tony rushed to the bed and took her pulse. It was slow but steady and the child was now breathing softly.

Basil entered the room a few moments later. 'I've told the parents,' he sighed. 'I think it's fair to say they're absolutely gutted. I wish I could have reassured them or given some hope for the future.'

The twins nodded while murmuring meaningless platitudes, unable to share the fact that, with a little luck and help from the angels, all would be well.

*****

Goth was raging with blind fury. Harry appeared with reinforcements shortly after they'd kidnapped Ninja.

'The Devil's not amused,' said Harry. He was terrified of the wrath of Goth, but even more so of his master if he didn't deliver the message.

'You're too fucking late you useless piece of shit.' She attacked him savagely.

Although it had been a while since he'd experienced such pain, Harry was glad the force of her second punch transported him into the ether at great speed. He didn't bother trying to slow himself or stopping, knowing that if he returned to her now, more of the same would follow.

Goth took her anger out on those who were left behind. Before long she was on her own. Her anger was nowhere near spent but she was exhausted from the fighting. Knowing she would be ineffective in her current state, she decided to rest for a while, before finding and torturing more unfortunate souls.

*****

Job done, Gabriella was delighted with the way it had gone. If the rest went to plan, Daisy would still sleep for a while but when she awoke, would remember nothing about her experiences with Goth-Roach, or the other angels. She would also start calling herself Ninja again. Most evils would move on to an easier target, but knowing Goth-Roach as they did, they expected her to make an appearance and cause havoc with Ninja and her family. Gabriella therefore allocated two guardian angels to look out for the child. They would watch over her twenty-four hours a day with the situation being reviewed every few months.

It had been decided to return the soul of Val to Cherussola and send her to sleep until a suitable host could be found. As Gabriella returned and touched base with Claire and Raphael, she discovered they had done exactly

154

that, but poor Val had been confused with no sense of who she really was. Her memories were mixed of her time as a troubled adult and a nervous and worried child. As the mission had been a lot easier than expected, none of the angels were particularly tired. Gabriella therefore started looking for a host for Val straight away. Unsure whether Goth-Roach would still be lurking, she decided to take Claire and Raphael with her. They would support if an attack happened and if all went well, Claire could visit her family.

Gabriella held onto Val's soul as the three angels watched the scene below. It was one they'd seen many times before but in many different environments. Three women stood around the peasant woman speaking soothing words of encouragement. She crouched down and was panting heavily. Gabriella knew it wouldn't be an easy life, but if Val could do the right things during the course of this life, it would be her final hardship and she'd be able to move on to eternity. As the baby girl slithered out of her onto the blanket below, Val's soul was transported into her body. She would remember nothing of her former existences.

Raphael and Claire said their goodbyes then Gabriella disappeared with a whoosh, to report her success back to the Committee. To say that Claire was curious about her family's meeting that weekend was an understatement.

Raphael took her hand in his and they headed for Marion's apartment.

Chapter 14

The twins, Fiona, Basil and Spike arrived at Marion's apartment the following Saturday. They were waiting for Marion to start the conversation about the school, but she decided to leave it to one of the others, assuming they had a plan. They didn't. Claire arrived and noticed the discomfort of everyone, except her mother. Spike barked and wagged his tail. Tony called him to heel and he obeyed, but kept a watching eye on the stranger with wings. Claire was laughing at the situation. It was infectious and Tony couldn't look at his brother for fear of laughing himself. Jim coughed inappropriately again and Marion tutted.

'You seem to be making a habit of this, son.'

'Sorry, mum, it's just that...' he couldn't hold it in any longer so the laughter was a relief. Tony joined in and it wasn't long before their mother, Basil and Fiona were all laughing. It was the first time Tony had laughed properly since Libby's departure. Basil decided to broach the subject of the school as soon as they all calmed down.

'Marion I am so sorry I couldn't tell you I work with Tony and Jim. Seeing them here that night at dinner was a surprise to us all and we've been looking for a way forward since then.'

'It's only because we're legally obliged to say nothing that we couldn't,' said Fiona. 'Technically, I broke the Official Secrets Act by divulging that they work together.'

They waited nervously for Marion to speak.

As she watched Claire was glad to see her mother was still loved and respected. Her boyfriend appeared to care for her and Claire was keen to discover how keen he really was.

She noticed the twinkle in her mother's eyes before her visitors.

'I'm not amused, with any of you, that you hid your situation from me, but I do understand why you had to do it.'

Claire thought her mother looked like a politician giving her acceptance speech. She was milking it so much.

'But I am looking forward to the future.'

Now they knew they could discuss parts of their jobs and all would be well. The tension in the room disappeared and they started to breathe easy again.

'You may all wish to know that I've decided to accept a position at the school. Tony, be a darling please and open the champagne. This calls for a celebration. It's just a shame Libby isn't here.'

'I know, mum. Even if it wasn't for the job I think it's a good idea to relocate. It can't be easy for you, knowing that Val jumped from here.'

'I'll get the drinks,' said Jim. Champagne felt inappropriate now the mood had changed while they talked about Libby and Val.

'How does everyone else feel about moving?' asked Marion.

'It would be easier for me,' said Basil. 'And from a selfish point of view it means I'll see more of you, my darling,' he kissed Marion. Fiona rolled her eyes and the twins looked down.

'We've already talked about it. Fiona and I have looked at a few places on the outskirts of Edinburgh.'

'Tony?'

'I liked the places Jim showed me and am going to put our house up for rent until I hear from Libby. I could do with a fresh start. And as for this little fella,' he tickled Spike. 'We have plans for him.' A look passed between Jim and Tony that only their mother picked up on. She briefly wondered what they were planning.

'I'm going to do some work with the dog section and he's going to be one of our working dogs when he's a little older.'

The glasses were filled and Marion held hers up.

'A glass of bubbly,' she said. 'Then the taxi will be here. To the future, whatever it holds.'

157

Claire smiled as her brothers looked up and winked when their mother wasn't watching. Basil was and it wasn't the first time he wondered about their strange behaviour.

Claire was still about later when they returned from the restaurant. With the exception of Marion they were tired from a hard week in work. The twins and Fiona said goodnight.

'Nightcap?' asked Basil and Marion opted for a vodka. He got her drink and poured himself a whisky with ice. Marion was shaking as Basil knelt in front of her. He took her hand.

'I love you, Marion. I've loved you since the first day I met you and I always will. Will you do me the honour of being my wife?'

He stood up and she followed suit. 'Yes, oh yes,' she flung her arms around him. 'I feel exactly the same. I adore you, Basil.'

Claire put her hand to her mouth and watched as they kissed slowly, savouring the moment and each other. She cried tears of happiness for her mother, so happy that she had at last found the love she deserved. A love like she shared with Raphael. 'He's perfect for you, mum,' she whispered.

Marion looked up. 'We have Claire's blessing you know. She's happy for us.'

'Of course she is, Marion.'

Marion knew he didn't believe her and didn't mind. She'd sensed her daughter's presence as she had when she'd first died. 'Thank you, my angel,'

Claire smiled down on the couple and plucked a feather from her wing. Her mother gasped as it floated to the floor. Basil was suitably surprised until the logical side of his brain took over. It had been a windy day and the feather must have blown in when they returned from dinner. If it meant Marion was happy, he didn't mind what she believed.

Even though she knew her mother couldn't see her, she blew her a kiss before wiggling her wings and disappearing with a whoosh. She found Raphael waiting for her and they made their way to their own home.

Chapter 15

Libby and Cassie were out on the boat they'd hired. The sea was calm as they watched the sunset. The sky was a mixture of oranges and pinks as the sun started to disappear beyond the horizon. A pod of dolphins unexpectedly appeared and entertained them for a few minutes. It seemed to Libby they had no reason for jumping out of the water and spinning in the air, other than for the pure enjoyment of it. She clapped her hands together and laughed, any angst or other problems diminished by the dolphin show. Then came a light-bulb moment and she stopped laughing. She should be sharing this with Tony, not her mad, unpredictable but lovely friend Cassie. Confused for such a long time, she now knew exactly what she wanted. She hoped Cassie didn't think she'd been stringing her along, as she found her incredibly attractive and, at one time, thought she did want a relationship with her. Now was the time to put a stop to it and tell her the truth. During their trip she'd discovered that Cassie had a temper so hoped she would understand and not kick off. They were due to dock within a few days and now her mind was made up, Libby was determined to do the right thing. As soon as possible after they docked she would phone Tony to ask his forgiveness and for him to take her back. She would beg if necessary. She might even ask Cassie if they could go ashore earlier than intended. Now her mind was made up, she wanted to act on it as quickly as possible. She hadn't spoken to her husband since she'd left. Libby closed her eyes and hoped with all her heart it wasn't too late.

It had been hard for Cassie to prepare everything without letting the cat out of the bag. It was a small boat with a cosy dining area. She'd lied earlier and told Libby she had a migraine and needed to be left alone. Libby had done as asked and left her in peace. Now the table was set, all ready for a romantic dinner for two. Although they had kissed on a drunken night out, that had been a few weeks before and Libby had avoided her advances since then. Cassie had given her space, certain it was only a matter of time before they'd be a proper couple. She judged, that time was now.

'Are you ready for dinner?' asked Cassie after the sun went down. She hoped it wasn't the only thing going down tonight and chuckled to herself.

'What's the joke?'

'I'll explain later,' Cassie replied. 'Follow me, I have a surprise.'

'I take it you're feeling better now.'

Cassie said she was and asked Libby to close her eyes as she guided her down the narrow stairs to the lower deck.

'Da na,' she said as Libby opened her eyes.

She looked at the cosy romantic set up. Cassie had obviously gone to a lot of trouble but had the totally wrong end of the stick. It was going to be awkward.

'Cassie, I...'

Cassie stopped her with a kiss.

'No, Cassie,' she pushed her away a bit harder than intended and Cassie banged her head on the door. 'I really like you, but as a friend. I love Tony and I'm going to ask him to take me back. I'm so sorry, Cassie. It's not that...'

Libby carried on talking as Cassie zoned out. She felt like she'd known this woman all of her life though it had been less than a year. She'd shared her most treasured secrets, shared her life with her, given her everything and even stolen to make their trip more memorable. On top of all that, she had listened to every boring story about Libby's husband and about her mother's death so many times, that she felt she'd been there herself. And this was how she was being repaid!

The red mist came down.

The first thing that came to hand was a heavy saucepan. Libby's scream and the shock on her face as her friend hit her with all the hurt of the last months, didn't stop her. By the time she had worked off her anger, Libby was silent and her face was hardly recognisable. Cassie cried as she dragged the dead weight up the stairs. She ran back down the stairs and into the store cupboard where she kept the diving gear. The belts had lead weights attached to them and the tears were still streaming as she tied both around Libby before pushing her over the side. They were in the Atlantic and there was not another vessel in sight. She was convinced the body wouldn't be found before the fish had cleaned all the meat off her bones. Cassie's tears were those of anger and hurt. Now fuming and heartbroken she knew it was nothing short of what Libby deserved. This had been the worst rejection ever. Libby was a flirt and a tease and wouldn't be able to hurt anyone else like she had her. Adrenaline still pumping, she ran back down the stairs and started clearing up the mess.

Absolutely shattered, she slept a deep sleep that night, not disturbed by guilt, remorse or regret.

*****

Spike had started howling earlier in the day and Marion was at her wit's end. She knew something was wrong with the puppy but couldn't work out what. After checking him over it appeared he wasn't in any physical pain. He hadn't been sick and wasn't displaying any signs of illness, but was obviously distressed. Unsure about whether to call the vet she decided to ring Tony first. Tony took the call, knowing his mother only contacted him during working hours if it was important.

'Libby?' he asked.

'No, son. I haven't heard anything. I'm phoning because Spike is really upset. He's been howling for most of the day and is really distressed. I wondered whether to call the vet.' She explained what she'd done so far.

'Let me talk to him, mum.'

'Really, Tony?

'I know it sounds ridiculous but isn't it worth trying before speaking to the vet?'

She shook her head but put the phone by the dog's ear so he could hear Tony. Spike stopped howling, and lay down. Marion moved the phone and as he listened to Tony, his tail thumped gently, but not with the enthusiasm he usually showed. When she eventually spoke to Tony again, Spike was still quiet and had closed his eyes.

'Well that did the trick, thankfully. It's like he's upset about something though.'

They talked for a little longer and agreed that Marion should take him to the vet the following day if he was still showing signs of distress.

'I'll try and get home a bit earlier tomorrow to pick him up,' Tony said before they said their goodbyes.

Spike wasn't howling the following day but wasn't his usual self either so Marion took him to the vet, just to be on the safe side.

'I can't find anything wrong with him, but he does seem lethargic for such a young puppy. We'll do a blood test to check that everything's as it should be and contact you with the results.'

Less than an hour after arriving back at the apartment, Spike started pacing and looking out of the window. Marion knew this signalled the arrival of his owner and, as promised, Tony arrived early. Spike seemed back to his usual self as he greeted him excitedly, but after the initial fuss was over, he cuddled into him and howled.

'What's the matter, boy?'

Spike answered him with more howling.

'See what I mean,' said Marion. 'This is what he was like from yesterday afternoon.'

'How peculiar. Maybe he's missing Libby?'

Spike's howling increased at the mention of her name. 'How strange,' said Marion as they looked at each other, bemused.

'I'll get him home, mum. But I don't want to leave him if I have to go out so can I bring him over for a bit tomorrow?'

Marion offered to help whenever Tony needed her and he was grateful he had such a supportive and loving family.

*****

Cassie spent the following two days clearing the mess and thinking of a legitimate story should any of Libby's family seek to contact her in future, then decided she would tell them Libby had decided to go back to her husband and she had no idea where she was. As long as all traces of evidence were removed from the boat, she believed she was home and dry; there certainly wouldn't be any evidence left in the sea. She returned to port as scheduled. Her first job was to buy new diving belts. Cassie laughed to herself, she could come up with a believable story about Libby's disappearance, but couldn't think of an excuse for the boat hire company, as to how she could lose the belts. They were common pieces of equipment and she was lucky enough to find a shop that sold the exact belts.

Carmo, the man they hired the boat from was giving it the once over before Cassie signed it in to him. His mate in the shop had already told him she'd purchased the new belts. He didn't mind, but was curious.

'Did you enjoy your trip?' he asked.

'Libby decided a life on the ocean waves isn't for her.'

He didn't smile. 'Where is your *girlfriend*?' He asked in broken English, but still able to emphasise the word girlfriend. They both knew what he inferred.

Cassie refused to bite, even though he irritated the hell out of her. 'She's got a headache and has gone for a walk,' she smiled.

'Well give her my best and I hope it doesn't spoil the rest of your holiday.'

'What happened to the old diving belts?' Carmo wasn't initially that bothered as she had replaced them but something about this woman wound him up. He became interested when she tried to mask her initial reaction.

'Libby dropped them over the side and we couldn't retrieve them, sorry. That's why she's not here today, she's too embarrassed to face you. I hope the new ones are okay? They looked the same to me as far as I could remember.'

164

His face didn't give anything away as she signed the paperwork and he took possession of his boat. His first job would normally be to get his workers to clean the boat, ready to hire out again, instead, Carmo told them to put it into dry dock and not to touch anything. He called his brother Earl, a sergeant in the local police force.

'I have a bad feeling,' said Carmo.

His brother trusted Carmo's instincts and agreed to keep an eye on Cassie.

*****

Possessions hadn't been Goth's preferred way of causing mayhem in the past. She didn't like the idea of fighting for headspace with someone else, and had seen how exhausting it could be. It was a specialised skill and not one she had wanted to pursue. Until now. Knowing this was currently the Devil's first choice, and the fact she was deep in manure with her master, Goth felt she had no option other than to learn this new skill. It had taken a while for her to be able to think clearly again. Her anger had turned from a red-hot fury to a slow burn that would take an eternity to extinguish. For her first outing she reverted to type. A busy supermarket with harassed parents and Friday afternoon queues. One woman was chatting and another was impatient to get past. Goth rammed the trolley of the second into the first. Although the woman apologised, a security guard had seen the incident and didn't want any trouble. He ejected her from the shop despite her protests of taking her business elsewhere. It wasn't a satisfying outcome for the evil so she looked for others. The same Friday night she cruised some pubs, deciding the crowd in the third would do the trick. The customers, mostly men, were watching the match and enjoying some friendly banter. Goth watched to see who was drinking the most and which ones would be most susceptible. She selected two and they made it easy for her. A drink was spilled and one of her targets refused to apologise for something he was determined he didn't do. When the other pushed into him it kicked off and a few punches were thrown. Before any major damage was done, their mates had

165

them under control. Both men were embarrassed and apologised to each other. Goth was mad that she couldn't even cause minor chaos, so went away to rethink her next move.

Later that same night, she was checking out the traffic on the motorways. It was dark and raining. She could see it took a lot of concentration for the man driving the mini-bus. The HGV truck he was stuck behind threw up lots of water and his wipers were on warp factor ten. The six children in the vehicle were happily sleeping, exhausted after their day out at the amusement park. The three adults were also tired. The two in the back were hoping nobody noticed they were getting fresh with each other, and the third was fighting sleep, his eyes opened every time his head jerked. Goth concentrated on the child who was asleep in the seat behind the driver. The adults were further back in the bus so she knew she had a chance. Although children were easier to possess she knew it wouldn't be a total breeze. As the driver checked his rear-view mirror and indicated to pull out she made her decision. Entering the child's head, the little girl hardly knew what was happening as she thought it was a dream. She wasn't even aware of what she was doing as she removed her seatbelt and forced herself over the back of the driver's seat. The driver was checking the traffic in his side mirrors as his daughter grabbed the steering wheel.

'Elizabeth, what the...' He was shocked at her strength and as he glanced up to take a quick look at her it wasn't her eyes that looked back. The adult who had been dozing came to as the vehicle jerked to one side, about to hit the truck it was overtaking. Although nodding off a few seconds before, he was now fully awake. As the children screamed he dived at Elizabeth and pulled her back. She screamed her fury then started to scratch and punch him, shouting words that would embarrass a seasoned soldier. Her father who was still struggling with the steering wheel over compensated and the vehicle veered into the fast lane. This part of the road was almost empty as the mini-bus hit the central reservation. Their world went into slow motion as the vehicle, now out of control, tipped over. Vehicles further behind careered on the wet road and two collided with each other as the mini-bus came to a stop, the wrong way up. Bodies were on top of each and in the silence, Elizabeth's voice rang out.

'Daddy help me.'

Goth left and hovered above as she watched the souls of the two adults in the back of the vehicle rise from their former bodies. A family of four in a following vehicle had also perished and she watched as those confused souls left their bodies too. She smiled at the outcome. Not a bad day's work and even better if those souls went to the dark side. She would have no say in that matter unfortunately. Chaos followed as a number of emergency vehicles arrived at the scene to treat the injured. She was happy with her efforts and tried watching further but was overcome by exhaustion, eventually giving in to it.

When she next woke, Goth wondered how a young soul like Ninja could keep possessing Daisy, but be significantly less drained than she was. She knew she was far more powerful so something wasn't right.

'Is it safe for me to come back?'

Harry's voice broke her reverie. She was pleasantly surprised to see him after their last encounter, assuming he would have latched onto someone else by now. Perhaps he had a message from their master. She looked as he hovered uncertainly below her. It would be good to have a bit of company again and some fun too, she thought. She needed help for her plans to work and Harry would be ideal.

'I won't hurt you unless you've come to deliver me to the Devil or have more bad news?'

'Nothing of the sort,' said Harry. 'I thought you could do with some company and wondered what you're up to?'

It was as good as saying he was back with her. Goth smiled properly for the first time in ages. They were a team and as long as he knew she was always the boss, all would be well.

167

'Welcome back. I've missed your ugly mug and your annoying habits.'

'I haven't missed your beatings and temper tantrums,' he ducked as she took a playful swipe at him. Harry had spoken before thinking. He knew he'd sailed close to the edge with that insult and couldn't push it any further. He was amazed she hadn't inflicted any pain. She must have missed him too, which made him feel special. He couldn't remember how long ago he'd last felt this happy. Knowing her as he did, he reminded himself to think before speaking in future, this was one relationship he didn't want to ruin. Harry also knew he had to hide any feelings of contentment or happiness. If the Devil found out, the consequences were dire.

'Follow me, Harry.'

He did as bid and it wasn't long before a door appeared before them. It was black with a red knocker. Goth ignored the knocker and gave the door a push. It opened into a room and Harry was wowed at the sight. To him it looked like an upmarket Vampire's den. Everything was black and red, from the walls, the pictures on them, to the fittings and furniture. Then his eyes took in the black king sized four-poster bed adorned with red sheets and bedding. A black curtain made of netting hung from the rails at the side of the bed. Goth grabbed his face and chewed his bottom lip, before kissing him with a passion he had never known. The girls he'd slept with during his life had been as inexperienced as he was. Even the one who had given birth to their son, Big Ed. It was already obvious that Goth knew a lot more than he did and his erection felt so real that he groaned. As he started to undress she slapped him.

'I'm in charge,' she said as she pushed him onto the bed.

He watched fascinated as she removed her clothes revealing a body covered in tattoos. She stood up and twirled around, not self-conscious like the girls he'd known when he was alive, but delighting in her own body. The tattoo on her back was the most impressive. A true likeness of their master and Harry thought the Devil was actually looking at him.

Goth laughed. 'He does have that affect, doesn't he? He can't see us so all you have to do, Harry,' she unzipped his jeans. 'Is enjoy yourself.'

As Harry felt her mouth around his penis, he closed his eyes and knew he'd do anything she asked.

He felt every sensation and pain, even though he no longer had a human body. Later he was glad as he knew he'd be covered in cuts and bruises. She had taken him to places he didn't know existed but now she was all business again. Harry had always liked but feared Goth, now she became his obsession. He didn't realise he was her slave to do with as she wished.

They were still lying naked on the bed as she turned to him.

'I need to work on my possession techniques. How did you feel after your first time?' she asked conversationally.

'I've never done it,' he eyed her magnificent body as he answered and Goth followed his eyes, amused.

'Harry, pay attention.'

'I left it too late. The longer you've been without a body, the more draining it is. That's why it's better to get the new ones like Ninja. It's much easier for them. And the more practise you get the easier it becomes. I heard,' he added hastily when he saw the dark frown.

'So practise makes perfect,' she laughed. 'Do you want to practise something else, Harry?' She knew she'd feel better with company, when she returned exhausted from any future possessions. He had to be kept loyal and Goth now knew the exact way to achieve that.

Harry could hardly contain his excitement as she pushed him roughly onto his back. His nipples were the first to feel the pain of her teeth and he cried out in pain and ecstasy.

Chapter 16

The angels and their assistants were busy when Libby died. They were trying to restore good on Earth while the evils who had escaped from the cave were trying to cause as much chaos as possible. Libby was one of the souls who hadn't been met, or directed or dragged to either place. She was shocked having suffered such a violent death but also heartbroken that she'd been robbed of the chance to tell Tony how she really felt. She had no sense of time and no idea how long she'd been on her own before the first soul approached her. Due to her experience with Cassie, Libby was suspicious and untrusting of those who spoke to her. Unlike young Ninja, she floated away from those who tried to befriend her. She quickly cottoned on that the darker the light the darker the soul so hid herself away from groups of dark lights and did her best to ignore those on their own. Any bright shining lights she did see appeared to be on their way somewhere else and she didn't have the nerve to approach them first. After what seemed like forever, she decided to travel further afield. It was then she realised she could visit Earth. Libby was unable to find Tony or any other members of her family. For a while she watched other people getting on with the day-to-day business of living and again cursed the powers that be for cutting her life short, but most of all she cursed Cassie.

'Well, what have we here then?' she hadn't noticed the light. A man, Libby guessed he was in his late teens and, dressed in nineteen fifties style spoke to her. 'You look lost.'

'I'm fine thanks,' she carried on watching the family scene below her hoping he'd take the hint, but he didn't.

'They look happy, don't they?'

He pointed to the family below, two adults and three children, walking along the pavement. The kids appeared excited and were chattering away, but Libby couldn't hear what they were saying.

'I guess so.'

'Watch this.'

He disappeared and the next thing Libby saw was the young girl falling from the pavement into the road. It looked like she'd been pushed and her father acted quickly, scooping her up from the road before an oncoming car hit here.

She heard his laughter before seeing him again, which confirmed he wasn't someone she wanted to hang around with. Libby disappeared as quickly as she could. Recalling what he looked like she vowed to avoid the evil sod in the future, at all costs. She couldn't understand who would want to do that to a child, then remembered what Cassie had done to her. Tired from her outing she needed to rest, so returned to what she considered a safe part of the ether, hoping she'd be hidden until she ventured out again.

Once she rested she knew it was safer to stay put. Libby did so for a while but the pull of watching family life was too much for her. Her own had been taken away so quickly and she longed to watch other people doing what she could no longer do. More cautious this time, she headed in the same direction as before, but to a different spot. There seemed to be more traffic so Libby was careful to avoid the darker lights. She saw two bright lights in the distance so stayed where she was in the hope they would stop and give her guidance. She didn't know who was the most surprised.

'Libby,' said Claire. 'Why are you here? What's happened?'

'Claire? Is that really you?' she looked at the vision of loveliness in front of her and promptly burst into tears.

*****

Goth had Harry's full support during her next possessions. She decided to stick with targeting children until she became stronger and better at it. She also took Harry's advice of practising low-key irritations rather than big events like the car crash. She entered a house where a woman was issuing instructions to her husband.

'I do know how to look after them. They are my children too.'

'I know, honey,' she said before kissing him.

'Have fun.'

They said their goodbyes. He fed the boys as soon as his wife left then cleaned up the kitchen. Later, his oldest son was showing the toddler his drawings and he nodded off, wondering why women made such a big fuss of looking after kids.

A noise woke him and he walked into the kitchen. His youngest was screaming as he held out his right arm. From above the wrist to the elbow his skin looked red raw and was dripping with water. His face was contorted with pain. The oldest was holding a kettle with steam coming out of it. He looked confused, not guilty.

'Oh Jesus, Sean. What have you done?'

Goth had already floated out of the body. She felt less tired this time but Harry was there to meet her. He held her in his arms then took her to the bedroom where she rested. When she came round he begged for her body but she refused.

'Soon, Harry. Find me another child first.'

He did as told and more misery was doled out to other victims and their families until Goth was satisfied she was good enough to move on to an older person. Harry got his reward. As they lay sated she told him her plan.

'I'll follow her for a while, so I know her routines and habits. Then I'll strike.'

'What do you need me to do?'

'Anything I tell you.'

*****

The unsuspecting twenty year old had no idea her life was about to take a turn for the worse.

Mel had finished her course work for the week and was looking forward to the weekend. Some of her friends were going to the student bar but she was tired. Dean would be over following his football match so she decided to watch a few crime shows to give her brain a rest.

She was nodding off a little while later, but something jerked her awake. There it was again. She felt a presence in the room and knew it wasn't her imagination.

Something weird was going on. She'd had this feeling many times during the past month or so, and felt like she was being watched or studied even. Mel went to the bathroom, trying to shake off whatever it was but it wouldn't go away. Deciding she did need company after all, she took off her pyjamas and dressed in jeans and a jumper. About to make her way to the bar, Mel felt as if something were pushing itself into her head. Her family were unaware of her studies into paranormal psychology. Marion's good friend Val had spooked her before she died so Mel had decided to do a little research. She'd read four case studies to get an understanding of the subject and it was quite scary if she did believe what had been written. Even more frightening, cases of child possession were all over the media recently, due to shocking criminal acts by children who had previously been as good as gold. The feeling she had now was exactly what was explained in papers she had read.

The first thing was to remain calm. It wasn't easy when believing an angry dead person was trying to get inside your head, but Mel did her best. The second was to think of material things, and the third was to be active. The fourth, which she hadn't read anywhere, was to call for help. Whenever her parents were unavailable or she didn't want to worry them, Auntie Marion was always the next port of call. She knew Marion would listen to her but would then tell her to pull herself together. There was no way Mel was calling Dean about this – she didn't have mental health issues and did not want the man she loved to think she did. She looked at her watch. He would be with her shortly anyway, so she had to get rid of whatever or whoever was trying to get inside her head. As one of her scarves lifted off the back of the chair and floated towards her, Mel knew she had to act quickly. She grabbed her phone and left the room. As she walked down the corridor she dialled her brother's number. It rang a few times and Mel started to feel strange. She tried to concentrate on her phone but then heard a voice that sounded vaguely familiar.

'Surprise! I was just coming to get you. I'm early because I...' Dean stopped talking as he looked at Mel. He had the strangest feeling that somebody else was looking at him.

'What the?' he said as he approached her. 'Mel. What's...'

'*Mel? What's happening? Speak to me...*' said the voice on the phone which Dean recognised as one of her twin brothers. Distracted, he looked at the phone. Mel held it in her left hand, with her arm outstretched. She smiled at him but it wasn't the smile he was used to. He didn't see her other arm move until it was too late. She grabbed his right arm by the wrist, in a vice-like grip. Dean screamed in agony as she twisted his arm. He felt sick as he heard the bone snap and shook his head, trying not to pass out with the pain. This creature in front of him wasn't his Mel. She possessed some sort of superhuman strength and he had to get away. She looked confused for a second and he took advantage by grabbing the phone out of her hand. Panting as he ran along the corridor, he spoke to her brother. 'Someone or something is inside Mel. It's broken my fucking arm. I know this sounds ridiculous but I've seen it with my own eyes. Oh fuck, she, it's coming after me. I'm not sure what I can...'

'Listen to me, Dean,' said Jim, trying to calm him down. 'I can get someone there to help but you have to stop her. Do you think you can do that?'

'I'll go to the bar and get help.'

'No, Dean. Nobody else is to know about this unless you want the press to get hold of it, or even worse, for Mel to be Sectioned. Talk to the Mel you know, about the good times you've had and the things you've done together. Get her back, Dean. You can do it. I'm going to ring off now. I'll get someone there as soon as I can. One more thing. When you know Mel's back with you, don't let her sleep okay? This is really important. She'll probably want a stiff drink after her experience but don't allow it, make her drink coffee. I'll get you some medical attention too, just hang in there until my guys arrive.' Jim rang off and Dean was too panicked to wonder how he knew so much about the subject. Mel was heading towards him and he could see some sort of internal struggle going on. His initial plan was to disable her by knocking her out with anything he could get his hands on. Now he knew he couldn't do that as Jim, or was it Tony, said she had to stay awake.

He started talking, trying to get her attention. 'Remember Spain, Mel. How much you loved it there. What we got up to on that secluded beach. Remember the feel of the sun on your face, the breeze and the sea. You said it was your idea of heaven.'

She smiled and it was his girlfriend smiling at him, not whoever else was inside her head.

'It was wonderful,' she said. Then her mouth contorted and she struggled to keep control of it.

'Stay with me, Mel. Get out of her you bastard.' Her brother hadn't told him to speak to the ghost in her head but that had just come out. Besides for an obvious struggle going on, there wasn't any other response.

'She's tired, Dean. I can feel it. But I'm tired too. I think I'll just have a little snooze.' She closed her eyes and bowed her head.

'Nooooooo,' Dean shouted and the shock made Mel's head jerk upwards. He was so glad it was a Friday and the other students were either in the bar or away for the weekend. 'Stay awake, Mel. Help will be here soon, I promise.' Now that the violence appeared to be over, he felt more comfortable talking to her. But as the situation calmed, his adrenaline started to dissipate reminding him of the pain in his arm. He tried his best to ignore it.

Goth had done as much as she could with the possession on this occasion. With one final boost of energy she left Mel's body. She went to Mel's room to deliver one final surprise then returned to watch the couple. She was now as tired as her host, if not more so. The fight had left her so she knew there was no point hanging around if she couldn't impose her will on the girl or anyone else. She'd given too much of herself and also knew that if they encountered any angels or their like on the return journey, Harry would need to fight them alone. The door Dean was standing next to shook as Goth rose up as quickly as she could. The strain left Mel's face and she slumped to the floor. Dean put her phone in his pocket and rushed towards her.

'What happened? And your arm! You must be in agony, let me have a look.' She tried to get up but collapsed again. 'I'm so tired. That was like all of my nightmares rolled into one. It's coming back to me now. She was in my head, Dean, fighting for control.'

'Come on, Mel. You have to get up. We can talk about all of this later.'

'I just want to lie down, I'm so....'

Her eyes were flickering again. Dean knew drastic action was required. 'You broke my bloody arm.' It was the most shocking thing he could think of to say to her and it did the job. Now fully awake her mouth opened and closed like a human fish.

'Oh, Dean. I'm so sorry. You know it wasn't me, don't you? I can't get my head around this. This is what must have happened to Libby's mother you know. But nobody believed the poor woman. They all thought she was mad. What if they think I'm mad?'

'I know you're not and so does your brother apparently. Come here.' He put his left arm around her, the right hanging useless by his side.

Her phone rang. It was Jim and he knew the evil had left her as soon as she answered.

'Mel, you're going to have to take time off. I've made some arrangements.'

'So you do believe I was possessed then?'

'Of course, and it's not only you.' They both knew he was referring to the recent incidences of so called devil children, where the parents or those close to them claimed they were possessed.

'Mel, Tony and I have...' he hesitated while deciding how much to tell her. 'Let's just say we have our own ideas on the subject and whatever's going on, we're not going to allow anything bad to happen to you.'

'I'm frightened.'

'Put your phone on loud speaker so I can speak to you and Dean at the same time.'

He waited until she had done as instructed then spoke. 'It's important that Mel stays awake and active, it appears it's harder to be possessed when you keep busy, so make some coffee and keep busy until my people arrive. They should be with you within a few hours. Do not drink any alcohol, Mel, even if the shock of what's happened makes you feel like a drink. Can you do that for me?'

'Yes, definitely.'

'I'm going to make arrangements for you to stay elsewhere, where people can help you through this, okay?'

Mel breathed a sigh of relief. '

It's essential that you keep active. Whatever you do, do not go to sleep. Do you understand?'

'Yes, Jim. Thanks.'

'You need to get to the hospital, Dean.'

'I'm okay,' he said through the pain. 'I'm not going anywhere until Mel is sorted.'

That was exactly what Jim wanted to hear.

They hung up and although frightened, she felt easier knowing that Dean was with her.

'You're not taking me without a fight,' Mel said out loud, looking upwards.

In the bar they said Dean had been mugged on his way back from football. He told them they'd already called an ambulance. They ordered coffees and waited, while chatting to friends.

As promised, Jim called back a little later. 'Where are you?'

'We're in the bar.'

Mel moved away from the people they were talking to and Dean followed.

'Right. Stay there until you see a couple come in. The girl has long brown hair with a ponytail tucked through the gap in her baseball cap. The guy has short ginger hair. As soon as you see them, head for the exit and wait outside. They'll be with you in less than a minute.

'It's all a bit cloak and dagger,' said Mel.

Jim knew she was frightened but also heard the excitement in her voice. *Good* he thought. *The adrenaline would keep her buzzing too much to want to sleep.* 'They will accompany you to your room. I want you to pack whatever you need for the next few weeks and include some of your study work.'

'Two weeks? Where are they taking me, Jim, and what's the plan?'

'Tony and I are in Scotland. We're going to look after you to make sure you don't come to any harm. John and Jane will travel with you. You can trust them both.'

'John and Jane? Seriously?' she saw two people enter the bar and didn't wait for her brother to answer. 'Oh, here they are now.'

'Right, Mel. Have an uneventful journey and don't worry about anything. Okay?'

'See you later, Jim.'

He'd already terminated the call and she rushed out of the door, explaining to Dean as she went. As her brother had promised John and Jane were waiting for her. They introduced themselves.

'Jim said I need to pack. Now you're here can we call an ambulance for Dean?'

'We'll drop him at A and E on our way,' said John. 'Let's get going.'

'You can wait here if you like. Dean will come with me and I'll be quick,' said Mel, noticing the look that passed between them.

'We'll come with you, Mel,' it was Jane speaking this time. 'Your room might not be as you left it and it can sometimes be a shock when...' She stopped talking as Mel rushed in front of them.

Her hand flew to her mouth when she opened the door. It looked as if a hurricane had hit leaving destruction in its wake. Her belongings were strewn all over the room

178

and anything that could be broken was. John made a call and Jane started to tidy up as Dean did his best to console Mel.

'Why me and who's doing this?'

They couldn't answer the question so Jane made soothing noises then asked Mel to pack what she could as quickly as possible.

'A clean-up team will be here shortly,' said John. 'They'll do a fire drill first to evacuate the building.'

'You've obviously done this before,' said Mel. 'How many people are affected?'

'Don't concern yourself with that,' said Jane. 'I'm sure your brothers will answer all of your questions when we get to Scotland.' Jane had no idea what Mel would be told. Her orders were to get the girl out of there ASAP and to keep her occupied. She'd seen one of the possessed youngsters so knew what they were dealing with. Flying was a risk but they'd ensure she was strapped in and a few of the others would be on the same flight.

Goth watched from above as they started their journey. Harry recognised her dark rage and moved out of reaching distance.

'Get back here,' she screamed with a burning desire to take her anger and frustration out on him.

He declined but tried to calm her, even though he knew it was pointless. 'It's only a minor setback, it'll all work out. Let's share each other then we can try again...'

Even though she was exhausted, her anger gave her a boost of energy. She was too fast for him and was all over him like a rash, punching, kicking and even biting. Harry couldn't escape from her so curled up to protect himself as much as he could. Exhausted and spent, she looked at him. For a moment Harry saw no evil in her eyes. The look was the nearest to remorse he had ever seen.

She held out her hand and he took it without hesitation. 'Come.' They sped off into the darkness, to her lair where she slept, then inflicted even more pain on him. But this time of the pleasurable kind.

Dean's arm was in a plaster and he'd been told not to play any sport until the plaster came off, hopefully six weeks later. As he returned to his digs he knew he'd have plenty of time to ponder and he wondered why his niece and girlfriend had been the targets of evil spirits. The whole experience had spooked him. The two friends he shared with were slouching on the sofa watching a classic match and Dean was relieved not to be on his own. They said hi and asked about his arm. Dean told them a vague story about being mugged then his phone rang. His roomies went back to watching the match and he was relieved to see it was Mel, so headed for his room.

'I know it's late, did I wake you?'

'I'm just back from the hospital. Out of action for six weeks. How are...'

'Oh, Dean, I'm so sorry. I can't believe this is happening to me and that I did that to you.'

He heard the fear and panic in her voice and wished he could be with her. Jim had called when he was at the hospital, to explain that it would be better for both of them if they didn't see each other during Mel's treatment. He refused to say what that treatment involved, only that she would find it difficult and it would be easier without any outside distractions. He was going nowhere and had to reassure her.

'You didn't break my arm, Mel, it was the demon inside you. You're safe now and in the best place to get help. Your brothers won't let any harm come to you.'

'I know that but it's still scary,' she hesitated. 'Will you come to see me?'

'Yes of course,' he lied as Jim had instructed. But according to her brother, she might not even know what day it was over the next few weeks, never mind who had visited and who had not.

'Get some rest now, Mel. I love you and I'm here for you. Whatever happens, we're in this together.'

He hoped he meant it as they said goodbye and disconnected the call.

Her brothers decided to take it in turns to stay with her during the night. Mel slept like a baby when she eventually got to bed that night. Knowing that Tony was in the room with her helped, as did the fact that it was two o'clock in the morning and she was absolutely shattered. Unbeknown to any of them, the evil spirit that had possessed her was far too exhausted to cause any further mischief that night, and the following. She tried again on the third night. Goth was trying to be stealthy and entered her head when she was having a pleasant dream. Mel sat up in bed. Still sleepy she was confused and not sure whether she was still dreaming. Jim had nodded off on the chair next to her bed but a sixth sense alerted him to the danger. He jerked awake and looked at his sister. The eyes were definitely the windows to the soul and he knew straight away that those looking back at him didn't belong to his sister. As he reached over and pressed the panic button, he could see Mel's eyes changing so knew that his half-sister was already fighting for dominance against the evil spirit inside her. Her face contorted, showing the battle raging within.

'Help me,' she said in a voice that Jim didn't recognise.

Then a slow smile spread across her mouth and Jim knew the demon was winning this particular battle. He remembered Dean's broken arm and knew he couldn't match the strength on his own. Thankfully he didn't have to as Tony came rushing through the door with two big male guards and a female nurse. The nurse held a syringe.

At the sight of the party, Mel went ballistic. Leaping from the bed she balled a fist and punched one of the guards in the face. They all heard the crack and she laughed. A strange, hideous noise sounding like a hyena crossed with a crow. Although in pain, the guard grabbed the arm that hit him. Tony secured her other arm behind her back. She was livid and started kicking out. The four men managed to return her to the bed. While the two guards tied her limbs to

181

the bed posts, Tony lay on top of her which made their job easier.

'Fuck, you and your precious fucking sister,' said the demon.

Mel's mouth was the only thing Goth could use so she uttered obscenities and bit Tony's ear. He lifted his head up so she couldn't reach him so she spat at him instead. The phlegm landed on his arm and he cried out in pain as it burnt his skin and blistered straight away.

'Tape her mouth, quickly,' he shouted.

The nurse took gaffa tape and scissors out of her bag, approached the bed cautiously and did as ordered.

The demon shook her head and screamed silently. Still unable to move any other part of Mel's body, she tried to take her anger out on anyone near, but was totally immobilised.

The twins started talking to their sister. 'Remember when we first met, Mel, and what a shock that was to all of us?'

They recalled times they had enjoyed the most then spoke to her about her first meeting with Dean – she had bored them with the story a number of times.

Her eyes flickered and they could see their sister was again fighting for dominance against the evil.

'Mel, I want you to solve these problems for me,' said Jim. 'What's seven and five?' he asked, then pulled the tape off her mouth.

There was a smile and this time it was from his sister. 'Twelve, give me something more challenging.'

He did as asked and eventually, the demon gave up and left her host.

As she floated above her, she swore at them all but none of them could hear.

'I'll be back and you won't know what's hit you,' she said. 'I'll kill the fucking lot of you.'

None of them heard a word.

Mel had some aches and bruises the following day but understood why her brothers and the guards had to be rough.

The following night was quiet but Goth visited the night after, again in the small hours. Tony was on duty this time and there was much of the same. The possession was shorter than the previous one with the twins testing Mel's mental agility and general knowledge.

Deep down Goth knew she was fighting a losing battle. Trying to possess Mel was totally different to possessing children, or even the few other adults whose heads she had been able to get inside. During the first possession Mel had been frightened and this made her vulnerable and more open to Goth's demands. Her fear had since diminished and now she was angry. But it wasn't an anger that Goth had been able to use to her advantage, it was a controlled anger coupled with determination that nobody was going to take over her mind and body. Goth had convinced herself it was worth the effort but now the seeds of doubt were starting to spread. Unable to admit defeat and such was her hate for Claire's family, she decided to keep trying to overcome her target, even though the Devil's orders were to possess children.

Goth needed to ensure she was at her maximum strength so a week passed before her next visit. The staff at the school had learnt not to become complacent so Tony and Jim still carried out their regular nightly routine. Mel had become frustrated and now she felt stronger, asked about Dean on a daily basis. Her parents and Marion enjoyed receiving messages from her on Social Media, but now wanted to speak to her and the twins knew they couldn't fool them for much longer.

Mel woke up as soon as she felt the presence trying to wheedle its way into her mind and body. 'She's here,' she said.

Tony pressed the button then started asking Mel questions.

As much as Goth tried, she couldn't possess her mind or body.

Mel concentrated all her energies, feeling confident.

183

She knew she was stronger and couldn't be beaten on this occasion. The guards, the twins and the nurse watched as Mel kept reciting facts in her attempt to keep the demon at bay.

Goth was tiring quickly but kept at it until she felt another presence. She wasn't the only one.

'Get out of her, you bitch.'

The twins hid their surprise at hearing Claire's voice.

Already tired, Goth knew she couldn't fight Claire on her own and win. With Harry she had a chance, but only if they were both fighting fit. She cut her losses and left. Goth finally admitted it was a waste of time trying to conquer Mel. Harry met her and as they rushed to avoid contact with Claire, Goth was already devising a plan to cause the hated family maximum harm.

'She's left her,' said Claire.

'How are you, Mel?' asked Jim, even though they could all see she was less shaken than on previous occasions.

'I'm okay. She didn't win at all that time,' Mel smiled. 'I feel a lot stronger.'

'Fantastic. Tony and I have to take a call but we'll be back soon. The guys will look after you. Okay?'

She said it was fine so they left her room and walked along the corridors towards one of the storerooms. Tony unlocked the door. They entered and closed it behind them.

'Tony, I...'

'Libby,' Tony said. He leaned against the wall and slid down it. Sitting on the floor he pulled his knees to his chest, and hugged them. Jim sat quietly next to him as he sobbed his heart out.

Claire watched, her heart breaking for her brother. As he sobbed she wondered, not for the first time, how her brothers knew instinctively what she was going to say.

Eventually the sobbing stopped and Tony lifted his head. 'How?'

'I'm so sorry, Tony, but Libby was murdered by the woman she went away with.'

'Murdered?'

'They were on a boat and fell out because Libby said she'd made a mistake and wanted to come home to you. Her so called friend went beserk, attacked her with a heavy saucepan and threw Libby into the sea. She weighted her body down so she wouldn't float.'

'I was going to divorce her, Claire, but she didn't deserve that. Nobody does.' He was muttering to himself now, trying to make sense of the situation. 'Is Libby...can she?'

'Our paths crossed briefly but she's moved on now and I won't see her again. I know it's little comfort but she wanted you to know she loved you and hoped to give your marriage a second chance. She was sorry for leaving.'

'I'm going to hunt down the woman who did this and when I catch her...'

Knowing his reaction was understandable Claire didn't say a word. She also knew that Jim wouldn't let him do anything stupid.

'Where is she?'

'Being questioned by the police, but it's unlikely they will charge her unless they find enough evidence. I'm so sorry to be the bearer of bad news, but I couldn't keep it from you.'

'I had a feeling something was wrong, but couldn't put my finger on it. I can't see mum until I've come to terms with this. She'll know there's something wrong and I won't be able to explain it.'

'I'll tell her we're on a secret mission,' said Jim. 'We'll tell The Director and he can arrange something so we don't have to work with Basil either.'

'Good idea. I have to go now but I'll try to get some help with Mel.' Raphael was checking on Ninja's progress. She wanted to find him to tell him that Goth-Roach had tried to possess Mel, and to ask whether they could get anyone to keep watch over her.

'Look after Tony, Jim and I'll see you again soon.'

She left with her customary whoosh while Tony tried to get rid of images of fish feasting on his wife's body.

185

Chapter 17

Despite being questioned twice, Cassie denied any knowledge of Libby's whereabouts. Carmo's brother was frustrated. He knew she was lying but couldn't prove anything. It was then that Tony was contacted and he broke the news to his mother.

'I had a feeling something was wrong, mum. It's been bugging me for weeks.'

Marion held his hand. 'There's no proof, son. Libby's missing is all we know at the moment and there's always hope.'

'She's gone, mum. I just know it.'

Something clicked with Marion and she grabbed a paper to check the date.

'So Libby's so called friend returned the boat on the twelfth of May,' she wracked her brains. 'I remember that week.' Marion went to the drawer in the kitchen where she kept all of the bills.

'What are you looking for?'

'The invoice from the vet. Here it is,' she handed it to Tony. 'Remember when I called you at work to tell you Spike was upset and was howling all day? Well that started on the ninth of May and I took him to the vet on the tenth.'

'Are you saying that Spike knew something had happened to Libby, mum?'

'Well I can't think of any other reason for his behavior, and the vet couldn't find anything wrong with him.'

Even though he knew telepathy was possible between people, and that his dog was clever, he found this a bit of a stretch and said so.

'Spike always knows when you're coming home or when you're going to phone, Tony. I think it's fair to say he's tuned into you so maybe he has some sort of sixth sense that was tuned in to Libby too.'

The dog barked on cue. They smiled sadly and it

186

lightened the mood.

'And if you know deep down that Libby's no longer with us, perhaps he picked up on your emotions. Who knows?'

'It's something we'll never know, but Spike is an extraordinary dog. The fact is that Libby's not coming back. If they don't find any evidence she can be declared dead after seven years. But I know, mum.'

'What will you do, Tony?'

'I was going to divorce her but that doesn't mean I didn't love her. I'll take some time off work, pack up the house and make a fresh start when we move to Scotland. I spoke to Carl and he's absolutely devastated. He's talking about going to Portugal and hunting down Libby's killer...' Tony took a moment to compose himself. 'That's exactly what I wanted to do but that would mean more lives ruined. It's tempting though.'

Marion didn't have the words so she held her son, wondering why fate had decided to lay another devastating blow on her family. First her daughter, now her daughter-in-law. She had an overwhelming desire to hear Mel's voice.

'I need to speak to Mel.'

Tony lifted his head. 'Sorry, with everything else that's going on I forgot to tell you. I spoke to Mel yesterday, just before she went on her field trip. She's returning later this week so you won't be able to speak to her until then.'

It seemed a little strange but Marion didn't push it, knowing her son had enough on his mind.

*****

Sergeant Earl, Carmo's brother, was delighted when his boss told him the British Police had been in touch.

'They've issued a European Arrest Warrant. Cassie Blake has had a number of names,' he read from the list in front of him. 'Her thefts total over two million and they're still investigating.'

Earl looked at the sheet his boss showed him. They had no concrete evidence about Libby Sylvester though his brother now said that a saucepan was missing from his boat.

At least if Cassie Blake was returned to the UK, she would be imprisoned for her financial crimes and wouldn't be able to hurt anyone else for a long time. That's not what he called justice for the family, but Earl was pragmatic and something was better than nothing. His boss's voice broke his train of thought.

'The Minister's given his approval. Pick her up and put her in custody. As soon as we have her we'll tell the British and they'll arrange to collect her.'

Her studio flat was at the marina where the rich and privileged hung out. *How the other half live* thought Earl as he smiled at a group of well dressed women who sipped their Latte's as he walked by with his colleague.

He rang the bell of the ground floor flat. Cassie opened the door and folded her arms when she saw who it was.

'Not you again. I've told you I've no idea where Libby is.'

Sergeant Earl smiled. 'Elizabeth Yardley, I'm arresting you on suspicion of embezzlement, fraud, identity theft,...'

It had been years since anyone had used her given name. Cassie was the name her sister had called her, saying that she just didn't look like a Liz, Beth or Elizabeth, so it was good enough for her latest identity. She was getting over the shock of being called Elizabeth when she started to listen to the charges. She attempted to close the door but the female police officer put her foot into the gap and grabbed her.

'Are you going to come quietly?' she asked in perfect English. Having nowhere to run to Cassie had no choice. She closed the door closed behind her. Sergeant Earl and his colleague guided her along the front towards their car. He nodded towards the luxurious looking vessels in the marina.

'Take one last look at this lot. Your long term future will be seen through the bars of a prison cell.'

She tried to shake his hand off her arm but the vice-like grip didn't budge. He gave her a smile, knowing she would be locked up for a long time.

Chapter 18

With the aftermath of Libby's disappearance, Marion and Basil postponed their wedding until the autumn. They were moving to Scotland but still planned to marry before relocating with Marion's side of the family. It was a sunny September day. As well as Marion's family, Basil's daughters were there with their families, the oldest having arrived from Australia two days earlier, as a wedding surprise arranged by Marion. They'd decided on a Civil Ceremony at Dordsey Manor; the country hotel they had used a number of times and were well known to the staff.

'It'll look great for the photos,' Marion had said to Mel. 'And besides, they know us well and will give us a good deal, I hope.'

Always practical and organised thought Mel as she followed her second mother up the aisle. The possession hadn't happened since the last time at the facility in Scotland. She had been left alone for months now so they all hoped that was the last of it, but nobody was certain. Her brothers were still wary because of the occasion and also because Claire had advised that one-off attacks were still possible, though unlikely. They had therefore insisted that guards attended the function and the three men discreetly blended in with the guests in different areas of the room. Her brothers were also watching out for her and so was Dean. Although Auntie Marion's wedding to Basil was meant to be a low-key event, she'd still wanted bridesmaids. Marion looked gorgeous in her lacy cream suit and Basil looked very distinguished in his light grey suit with faint light pink stripes. Mel loved her own purple tight-fitting dress. Fiona's was a similar style to Mel's but bright red, while one of Basil's daughters wore a green satin dress and the other was in midnight blue. Instead of clashing Mel thought it somehow worked and they complemented each other. She took a sneaky look at the man she loved as the bridesmaids followed Marion up the aisle and he smiled. Instead of being wary of her he had known she was telling the truth and had vowed to stand by her, whatever the future held, despite her breaking one of his arms when the evil woman was in her head. That seemed so long ago now and she was relieved his arm had healed without any lasting damage, and he could still play his beloved football without any problems. She was also more relaxed knowing there was discreet security at the wedding, in case the evil soul decided to try to ruin the day. She did wonder how long it would take her to feel completely safe again, but as long as she remained strong and had her boyfriend and brothers on her side, nobody could take over her mind or body.

Concentrating on the occasion, Mel took Marion's posy and sat down next to Dean, while Fiona sat next to the twins and Basil's daughters with their own families on the other side of the aisle. Marion was glowing as she said *I do*. The guests laughed as Basil picked her up and swung her around. It was a perfect day so far and Mel had never seen Marion so happy. They clearly adored each other. She looked at Dean and he smiled and squeezed her hand. She hoped they would still be as much in love when they were that age.

The ceremony over, the bride and groom went to sign the register as their guests waited for their return. There was spontaneous clapping as they walked back down the aisle towards the exit. Those that knew breathed a sigh of relief that Mel hadn't received some unwanted attention.

The happy couple greeted each guest as they exited the manor then everybody made their way to the outskirts of the woods on the path of red carpet laid by the staff. Some of the photographs would have the countryside as a backdrop, the Manor would be in the background of the others. As a breeze whipped up a few clouds scudded towards the sun so they knew to make the most of the good British weather before it changed.

*****

Goth was bored and ready for some action. She'd been waiting with Harry while the ceremony took place and now she just wanted to get on with her plan and watch as

191

this hated family got their comeuppance. Claire had avoided her revenge so far and it was no longer safe or practical to possess Mel. Even though the angels were no longer with her constantly, Mel was mentally strong and that made it harder for her to be possessed. It had taken too much out of Goth and she knew if she carried on, it was only a matter of time before the angels would catch her exhausted soul on the way home and destroy her for good. To add to her fury, the small sense of triumph she felt after she had discovered her sister Cassie had dealt a blow to the family she despised by killing their beloved Libby, was long since spent. She was pleased her sibling had proven herself to be as evil as she was. That would guarantee they would meet again and Goth relished the prospect of teaching her younger sister the ways of the Devil. Sadly that wouldn't happen any time soon, Cassie was languishing in a London prison on an eight-year sentence. Goth wanted to pay back the world for all of her ills, which in her evil and warped mind started and ended with this family.

The wedding party exited the Manor and she turned to Harry.

'You know how important this is, and how much it means to me?' she asked.

'Of course.'

She took his face in her hands and pulled him toward her. Without warning she pushed open his lips and forced her tongue into his mouth. Harry felt his excitement reach fever pitch when she nibbled his bottom lip, then bit it roughly.

They heard the motorbike and she pulled away. 'Ready?'

'Yes.'

'Let's go.'

They headed towards the motorbike intent on causing pain and chaos, totally unaware they weren't the only uninvited guests at the wedding.

The biker was in his element. This was his last job and after delivering the package to the Manor it was a thirty minute ride to the depot where he'd pick up his car and head for home for a night of bliss with his girl. Singing his favourite song in head, he first realised something was wrong when it felt like someone else was trying to sing an old song instead.

'What the hell?' he said out loud when the bike veered off course and headed for the women standing on the grass. The biker knew his own hands were steering, he tried to change direction when he felt a hand grab his crutch. Looking down at his leathers there was nothing to be seen but a hand was definitely playing with his jewels. He no longer cared as he'd lost consciousness and Harry had possessed him completely.

*****

They were taking their time so Marion was chatting to Mel while the men were having their photographs taken. The women heard the sound of a motorbike in the distance but thought nothing of it until the noise increased. Marion and Mel turned towards the sound as the bike was travelling at speed up the Manor's long driveway. It changed direction veering off the gravel onto the grass and they realised it was coming straight at them. The guards ran towards them but were too far away to help. Without thinking Marion pushed Mel out of the way, then her world went into slow motion. She felt herself falling to the ground and watched as the motorbike suddenly went off in another direction.

'You didn't think I'd let you go that easily did you?' It was Basil lying on the grass with her and she wondered how he'd got to her so quickly.

'Your boys wanted some photographs taken so I said I'd wander off to see how you were doing.'

They both got up slowly. 'Ouch,' said Marion as she felt a shooting pain in her foot. 'Look at the state of my suit.' She was covered in grass and muck, but wasn't overly concerned, knowing it could have been much worse.

'Whatever must have possessed the motorbiker to come straight at us?'

Possessed was probably the right word thought Mel as she hurried to see how Marion was.

'Are you all right? What a heroine you are putting me before yourself.' As Mel wrapped Marion in a hug, she wondered why someone would want to kill her. Then they looked up as the engine revved. Mel screamed as it headed straight for them again.

*****

Already alerted by the near miss, Claire and Raphael had stopped watching the photographer and moved near to Marion and Mel. They didn't need to discuss a plan as Claire approached the bike and Raphael the women. 'Good luck,' he said as she hurried away.

Harry didn't know what hit his host as the biker flew through the air and landed with a thud on the grass.

'So it's me and you again,' said Goth, though she knew she didn't have the power to control the bike and to overcome Claire. She left the bike and concentrated on her old enemy. Goth imagined how pleased her master would be if she took her prize to Hell. Years of hurt and anger welled up inside her as she recalled how this angel had caused the majority of her problems, and the humiliation she had to suffer as part Goth, part Roach. All sense of reason left her as Goth prepared her tired body for a fight. Knowing she would need Harry's help wasn't a problem as she had hooked him with the promise of eternal ecstasy.

The motorbike kept going for twenty metres before it lost momentum and fell on its side. As soon as Raphael knew the women were no longer in danger, he rushed to help Claire.

In her earthly life, and not long after she had left it, the urge would have been to inflict maximum pain on the evil spirit she knew as Goth-Roach. But not so as an angel. Despite the fact she was expected to be good, Claire also felt it. She did want the evil done by Goth-Roach to stop and she also wanted her soul to be diminished. She now thought of her as a somewhat pathetic and sad individual who would never know what it was to love and be loved, to feel the pure joy of giving and the intense delight of being surrounded by warm loving souls, who only wanted to make the world a better place. It was with this mind set that Claire and Raphael joined hands and formed a circle of love around Goth-Roach. While waiting for Harry, Goth started by taunting Claire.

'Your family is totally fucked up. What sort of man is your brother when his wife wants to be a lesbian?'

Claire smiled serenely.

Goth tried another tack. 'You couldn't even find yourself a nice white angel eh?'

Raphael laughed as did Claire and Goth had had enough. She kicked out. They broke hands to avoid her kicks and punches. Although furious, she was tiring and none of her strikes connected. Her anger kept her going and it was a while before she found reason again, realising she was beat.

'Harry,' she called. 'Harry, help me.'

There was no response and as she looked up, she saw him hovering high above her. It hit her that her feelings for him were more than the need to possess and control, and she realised she felt love, or her version of love. As he moved further away, she acknowledged she was being let down again. Memories from her miserable life appeared in front of her like scenes from a movie and for the first time since death, she hated herself.

Claire broke her train of thought. 'Cockroach time,' she said with no joy in the words. Goth looked at her body as it transformed, this time from her feet up. She screamed, knowing there was no hope of a second escape from the horrendous cave.

*****

'What's happening?' asked Marion as they all looked up to the tree. Its branches swayed and the leaves drifted to the ground.

'Nothing,' said Basil. 'Let's get cleaned up so we can enjoy our reception. Have you got something to change into?'

195

Marion said she had and the married couple made their way to their room. Fiona was the only one who watched the twins as they looked up to the tree.

'Thanks, Claire,' said Tony, and Jim gave a thumbs up.

On her way to the cave with her lover and the ugly cockroach, their sister didn't notice.

Acknowledgements

Thanks to my husband Allan for listening (or doing a good job of pretending to listen), to my fabulous editor Jill Turner and wonderful cover designer Jessica Bell. Thanks also to all my friends for their support.

Another Author's Note

Thank you for purchasing this book. I hope you enjoyed reading it as much as I did writing it.

If you like what you've read so far, you may be interested in my other books:

Beyond Limits (The Afterlife Series Book 5)

Beyond Sunnyfields (The Afterlife Series Book 6) coming soon

Unlikely Soldiers Book 1 (Civvy to Squaddie)
Unlikely Soldiers Book 2 (Secrets & Lies)
Unlikely Soldiers Book 3 (Friends & Revenge)
Unlikely Soldiers Book 4 (Murder & Mayhem)

The Island Dog Squad Book 1 (Sandy's Story) - FREE AT THIS LINK
https://dl.bookfunnel.com/wdh6nl8p08

The Island Dog Squad Book 2 (Another Crazy Mission)
The Island Dog Squad Book 3 (People Problems)

Court Out (A Netball Girls' Drama)

Non-fiction:

Zak, My Boy Wonder

And for children:

Reindeer Dreams
Jason the Penguin (He's Different)
Jason the Penguin (He Learns to Swim)

Further information is on my website https://debmcewansbooksandblogs.com or you can connect with me on Facebook:

https://www.facebook.com/DebMcEwansbooksandblogs/?ref=bookmarks

About the Author

Following a career of over thirty years in the British Army, I moved to Cyprus with my husband to become weather refugees.

I've written children's books about Jason the penguin and Barry the reindeer, and books for a more mature audience about dogs, the afterlife, soldiers and netball players, along with a non-fiction book about a very special boy named Zak.

'Court Out (A Netball Girls' Drama)' is a standalone novel. Using netball as an escape from her miserable home life, Marsha Lawson is desperate to keep the past buried and to forge a brighter future. But she's not the only one with secrets. When two players want revenge, a tsunami of emotions is released at a tournament, leaving destruction in its wake. As the wave starts spreading throughout the team, can Marsha and the others escape its deadly grasp, or will their emotional baggage pull them under, with devastating consequences for their families and team-mates?

The Afterlife series was inspired by ants. I was in the garden contemplating whether to squash an irritating ant or to let it live. I wondered whether anyone *up there* decides the

4

same about us and thus the series was born. Book six is currently in the planning stage and I'm not yet sure when the series will end.

'The Island Dog Squad' is a series of novellas told from a dog's point of view. It was inspired by the rescue dog we adopted in 2018. The real Sandy is a sensitive soul, not quite like her fictional namesake, and the other characters are based on Sandy's real-life mates.

'Zak, My Boy Wonder', is a non-fiction book co-written with Zak's Mum, Joanne Lythgoe. I met Jo and her children when we moved to Cyprus in 2013. Jo shared her story over a drink one night and I was astounded, finding it hard to believe that a family could be treated with such cruelty, indifference and a complete lack of compassion and empathy. This sounded like a tale from Victorian times and not the twenty-first century. When I suggested she share her story, Jo said she was too busy looking after both children – especially Zak who still needed a number of surgeries – and didn't have the emotional or physical energy required to dig up the past. Almost fourteen years after Zak's birth, Jo felt ready to share this harrowing but inspirational tale of a woman and her family who refused to give up and were determined not to let the judgemental, nasty, small-minded people grind them down.

When I'm not writing I love spending time with Allan and our rescue dog Sandy. I also enjoy keeping fit and socialising, and will do anything to avoid housework.

Printed in Great Britain
by Amazon